Dane looked up at her, the bruises on his face purpling, yet they did little to detract from his good looks. He wouldn't have been out of place in the pages of a men's magazine, modeling hiking gear or adventure expeditions.

"You came back," he said. "I wasn't sure you would."

"Take me to where you've hidden the proof of what you've learned about TDC," she said. "I need those videos and photos to make my case to the Rangers."

"I'm not sure that's safe. I can tell you where I've hidden them, but you'd probably have to get a warrant to retrieve them."

"I'm not going to get a warrant on my secondhand account of what you've told me." She crouched down until she was looking him in the eyes. "All the talking in the world does no good without proof. I need that evidence."

He nodded. "All right. But it's going to be dangerous."

"I'm not afraid of danger."

PRESUMED DEADLY

Cindi Myers

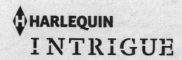

For Loretta and Jim.

HARLEQUIN®
INTRIGUE®

ISBN-13: 978-1-335-40166-3

Presumed Deadly

Copyright © 2021 by Cynthia Myers

This edition published by arrangement with Harlequin Books S.A.

For questions and comments about the quality of this book, please contact us at CustomerService@Harlequin.com.

Harlequin Enterprises ULC
22 Adelaide St. West, 40th Floor
Toronto, Ontario M5H 4E3, Canada
www.Harlequin.com

Printed in U.S.A.

Cindi Myers is the author of more than fifty novels. When she's not crafting new romance plots, she enjoys skiing, gardening, cooking, crafting and daydreaming. A lover of small-town life, she lives with her husband and two spoiled dogs in the Colorado mountains.

Books by Cindi Myers

Harlequin Intrigue

Visit the Author Profile page at Harlequin.com.

CAST OF CHARACTERS

Faith Martin—The Ranger Brigade's newest member almost died when she trusted the wrong man during her stint as a sheriff's deputy. She's determined not to make the same mistake again.

Dane Trask—In the weeks he's been hiding out in Black Canyon of Gunnison National Park, Dane has been viewed as a hero by some and a menace by many. Will Faith exonerate him or prove his guilt?

Larry Kempner—The IT specialist for TDC Enterprises contacts Faith and says he has information about Dane, but he dies before he can reveal that information. Was his death suicide or murder?

Mike Stacy—The fisherman claims he saw Dane Trask with Larry Kempner, but details of his story don't add up.

Charles Terrell—TDC's president is determined to bring Dane Trask to justice, but The Ranger Brigade suspects he has secrets of his own to hide.

Chapter One

From the back of the crowd, Dane Trask watched the woman who was speaking to the gathered reporters and members of the public. They stood in front of Ranger Brigade headquarters near the entrance to Black Canyon of the Gunnison National Park. A short, slender woman wearing the khaki uniform of the Rangers, she had drawn her dark hair back into a bun at the nape of her neck, a style that might have been severe on anyone with less delicate, feminine features. On Deputy Faith Martin, the effect was of a ballerina in disguise. The few stray curls the wind had tugged loose further softened her appearance.

She attempted to mask the softness with a straight back and shoulders, and a firm voice that carried authority. When she spoke, the reporters—and Dane—leaned forward to listen. "We are still searching for Dane Trask, and welcome any information from the public that could lead to his safe return," she said.

Several other Ranger officers and the commander, who stood behind Deputy Martin on the metal platform erected outside the building, shifted restlessly.

Every one of those men and women had been hunting Dane for the past seven weeks. What would they say if they knew he was here in this sun-lit parking lot, less than fifty yards from them?

Martin moved on to the main reason behind this press conference, the recent death of Terrell, Davis, and Compton vice president Mitch Ruffino in a shootout with Rangers and the Montrose County Sheriff's Office. "The evidence we have uncovered shows that Mitchell Ruffino, in his capacity as vice president of TDC Enterprises, falsified records to obscure the removal of radioactive material from land donated at his direction for a new elementary school," she said. "Dane Trask allegedly discovered this and confronted Ruffino, who threatened Trask and his family. Trask fled, and it was actually his daughter, Audra Trask, who uncovered the plot and worked with the Rangers to expose the crime."

Dane's chest tightened at the mention of Audra. She was here today, too, standing at the end of the line of Rangers, one hand clutching the arm of a blond officer who looked more like a surfer than a cop. She looked good, smiling and happy, probably relieved that this ordeal was over and she was safe.

If only Dane could believe that. His gaze shifted to the other end of the line of people on the dais, to the silver-haired man at the very end. Dressed in a gray business suit, Charles Terrell radiated power and success. Now that Ruffino was out of the way, Terrell had everything under control. He had said so in an article that had made not just the local and

Denver papers, but national news. "We are shocked and horrified that a man we trusted would carry out such a criminal scheme and we are determined to do everything in our power to set things right," Terrell had said in the copy of the *Denver Post* Dane had found at a campsite in the park. "We are working hard to regain the trust and confidence of communities we are a part of, and we're paying reparations to those victimized by Ruffino—and that includes Dane Trask. We hope Dane will step forward soon so that we can reward him for his efforts to expose Ruffino's crimes."

Yeah, Terrell wanted Dane to step forward, all right. So he could finish the job Ruffino had started.

"Is Dane Trask still a criminal suspect?" a reporter near the front of the crowd asked.

"Mr. Trask is still missing and we would like to find him," Martin said. She looked out across the crowd and Dane moved behind a taller man, instinctively avoiding her gaze, though he was sure no one would recognize him. Since disappearing into the wilderness of the park over seven weeks before, he'd let his beard and hair grow. Today he wore the braid, bandana and leather jacket of a biker, mirrored sunglasses to hide his eyes, stooped his shoulders to disguise his height. He was just another tourist drawn by the crowd near the park entrance.

"But is Trask still a criminal suspect?" the reporter asked again. "Is he wanted in the death of Roy Holliday, or for thefts from campers in the park, or for other unsolved crimes in the area?"

"Mr. Trask is not a suspect in the death of Roy Holliday," Deputy Martin said.

Dane had read about the reporter whose body had been found just outside the park—miles from anywhere Dane had been. But TDC had tried to make him the scapegoat for that and other of their crimes.

"Did Mitch Ruffino kill Holliday?" another reporter asked.

"Mr. Ruffino is a suspect in that case, yes," Martin said.

"Pretty convenient, now that he's dead," someone—Dane couldn't tell who—said.

"If Mitch Ruffino threatened Dane Trask, then now that Ruffino is dead, doesn't that mean it's safe for Trask to come out of hiding?" The speaker, a blond woman Dane thought worked for one of the local television stations, stood on her toes to see over the man in front of her.

"Yes," Martin said, "and we would very much like him to do that."

"Why do you think he hasn't come forward?" the first man asked. "Do you think he's still alive?"

"We believe he is still alive," Martin said. "As for why he hasn't come forward, I think Dane Trask is the only one who can answer that question."

"Is TDC still offering a reward for Trask's apprehension?" someone asked.

Martin looked to Terrell, who took a step forward and said, in a loud voice that carried, "We believe that since Dane hasn't yet come forward, he may not be aware that it's safe to do so. Or he may be hurt or injured. Therefore, we are increasing the reward to whoever finds him from twenty-five thousand dollars to fifty thousand."

A gasp rose from the crowd and the people around Dane murmured. But he was watching Martin. Her expression clearly conveyed that she hadn't been informed of this new development and she wasn't pleased. Not a smart move on Terrell's part, Dane thought. Why offer so much cash for a man who wasn't a threat anymore?

Because Dane was still very much a threat to Terrell and his operation. Was Martin asking herself that question, and would she come up with the right answer?

Her eyes shifted, and she looked right at him. He felt that gaze, even across this parking lot, like the hot sting of a thrown dart. He forced himself to remain still, to meet the look from behind the mirrored lenses of his sunglasses. She didn't know who he was. He wasn't Dane Trask, outlaw—he was just a biker who had caught her eye. He smiled, a slow, frankly lascivious look. She jerked her gaze away, but there was no mistaking the hot flush that swept across her cheeks.

Or the warm thrill of desire that gripped him at her response. No surprise there. He'd been alone a long time now, and Deputy Martin was an attractive woman. But he knew himself well enough to admit that it was more than her feminine beauty that got to him. When their eyes had met, something else had registered with him. Faith Martin was smart.

Smart enough to match wits with him. The idea

intrigued him. He'd have to be careful to avoid this one. She was too tempting—and there was too much at stake.

AFTER THE PRESS conference ended, Faith Martin followed the commander and her fellow officers and Audra Trask into Ranger headquarters, shutting the door behind her and shutting out the crowd still milling around the dais outside. Charles Terrell was still out there, taking questions from the press and glad-handing the public, determined to personally rebuild TDC's reputation, one person at a time. He would probably do it, too. He had that slick charisma that played well on television and in the papers. Some of it might even be sincere.

"I think that went well," Audra Trask, who had her father's chin and his dark hair and eyes but was much more slightly built, said. She smiled at Faith, though worry still haunted her eyes. "I hope Dad hears about it and shows up soon."

"Maybe he will," Faith said. She got that Dane Trask was Audra's father, so of course she was going to be worried about the man, but Faith had lost patience with him weeks ago.

"Good job out there, Martin." Faith automatically stood even straighter as Commander Grant Sanderlin approached. In the less than two months she had been with the Ranger Brigade, he'd proved himself to be both firm and fair. But he still intimidated her. He was FBI with years of experience and she was a deputy sheriff from a rural county. She'd been assigned as the liaison between the Rangers and local law enforcement, and though she was good at her job, no one was pretending she had as much experience as everyone else on the team. They still treated her like an equal, but she suspected they were mostly glad she was around to field inquiries from the press and handle paperwork.

"Thank you, sir," she said.

"Had Terrell mentioned the increased reward to you?" Sanderlin asked.

"No, sir." She frowned. "I'm not sure what he's getting at with that offer. If Mitch Ruffino originally offered the reward in the hope that someone would find Dane Trask before he blew the whistle on what Ruffino was up to, why would TDC continue to offer the reward now?"

"A lot of local people support Trask," Officer Mark "Hud" Hudson said from his position very close to Audra. The handsome blond officer and Dane's daughter had become involved during the hunt for her father and the romance showed no sign of abating. "They see him as a hero, taking on TDC even though the company threatened his life. Maybe TDC is hoping to garner public goodwill by supporting that idea."

As far as Faith was concerned, Dane Trask had run when he could have stood and fought, and instead of coming right out with what he knew about TDC, he'd left lots of cryptic clues that had made it impossible for local law enforcement to determine whose side he was on and what he was really up to. Not to mention, he'd stolen from campers and had killed at least one man. Granted, that man had been holding Trask's former girlfriend hostage and might have killed her, but still. Dane Trask was clearly no saint.

"I don't trust TDC," Audra said. "I know they said all of this—bribing officials and falsifying reports and everything—was all Mitch Ruffino's fault. But could Ruffino's bosses really have had no idea at all about what he was up to?"

Faith agreed with Audra. Then again, she wasn't in the habit of taking many people at face value.

"I think it's safe to say that TDC is going to be under the microscope for quite a while to come," Sanderlin said. "It may be that when Dane Trask does finally decide to come forward, he'll be able to shed light on all of Ruffino's—and possibly TDC's—illegal activities."

The commander returned to his office and the others went back to their desks, or to their assigned patrol areas for the day. The Ranger Brigade was responsible for law enforcement on the public lands in this part of Colorado—an expanse that included the national park, a national recreation area and a national conservation area. Their jurisdiction also included wildlife preserves, national forests, Bureau of Land Management and Bureau of Reclamation property—a big chunk of the state that was largely without roads, houses or people to notice who was up to no good. At various times the land had been utilized by criminals for everything from growing and processing illegal drugs, smuggling goods and people, stealing valuable artifacts or simply hiding from the law. The Rangers couldn't begin to cover all of the territory, but they had a good track record of zeroing in on major crimes and reining in the worst abuses.

But Faith was involved in very little of that. As Public Information Officer, she spent most of her time at her desk, writing press releases and fielding media inquiries. Occasionally, she was the public face of the Ranger Brigade, giving interviews or hosting press conferences. She carried a weapon and wore a badge like every other member of the team, but she didn't really feel like one of them.

"Who was the biker giving you the eye?"

She turned and Officer Carmen Redhorse moved in alongside her. Carmen, a member of the Ute tribe, was the only other woman with the Rangers. She had been with them from the very first, and was married to a Parks and Wildlife officer she had met on the job. Rumor had it she was a former beauty queen, and Faith could believe it. Carmen had long black hair and dark eyes with thick lashes, and the elegant profile of a model. And she was definitely a badass who could hold her own with anyone else on the force. She was a top marksman, and good at connecting the dots in tough cases. And she hadn't missed the brief exchange between Faith and the biker.

"Never saw him before," Faith said. "Just another jerk trying to get a rise out of a woman with a badge."

"I haven't seen him around before, either," Carmen said. "He's in better shape than most of the guys that ride through here—no beer gut on that one."

At Faith's raised eyebrow, Carmen grinned. "Hey, I'm married, not dead. I'm going to notice a built guy in black leather."

Faith felt her cheeks heat again. Yeah, the biker was built, all right. And though those mirrored shades had hidden his eyes, there was no missing the arrogance in the leer he'd sent her way. She liked a confident man, but not one who was full of himself. "It takes more than a body to impress me," she said. "The last thing I want is a gym rat who's dumb as a box of rocks."

"One thing about being a cop," Carmen said, "you learn how to handle trouble."

Right. Faith knew all about trouble. She had made a mistake exactly once, letting a man get the better of her. That was never going to happen again.

Chapter Two

Dane left the parking lot when the first spectators began drifting away. He debated lingering, maybe trying to get closer to hear what Terrell had to say. But he couldn't risk someone noticing him—and maybe noticing that he didn't have a motorcycle or any other vehicle.

And Terrell was probably just spouting the company line about being appalled at the crimes Mitch Ruffino had carried out without his knowledge, and TDC's commitment to making things right, et cetera. TDC would make a big show and throw some money around until they were back in everyone's good graces.

Then they would go right on raking in the profits from the side of their business no one talked about. Dane's biggest mistake had been confronting Ruffino with his findings about that "sideline" instead of going straight to law enforcement. Even with all his experience, he hadn't wanted to believe what he had discovered. Some part of him had hoped for a different explanation for what he'd seen.

Of course, there was no explanation that made

sense—except the one he had come to. TDC was a criminal operation, and Dane didn't for a minute believe the crime had started and ended with Mitch Ruffino. The number-one reason Ruffino was dead now was so that he couldn't reveal how deep the rot went.

And Dane and Audra and everyone else he loved were only alive because he had run. Some people thought he was a coward for that, but he cared more about staying alive.

And he cared about continuing to fight. He could make all the accusations against TDC he wanted, but until the right authorities uncovered the evidence for themselves, TDC wasn't going to be stopped. One man's word was never as good as solid proof Terrell and the others couldn't hide.

He slipped past the row of cars at the far end of the parking lot and walked the path toward the visitor center, where a row of motorcycles was parked. He followed a walkway around the building to a scenic overlook where people gathered for their first glimpse into the Black Canyon—a deep fissure that revealed a landscape of painted rocks and shadowed habitat beneath the harsh desert above.

From the overlook, a path led along the rim of the canyon. Dane moved past the clusters of tourists, until he had left them all behind. Then he cut over to a different trail, a steep descent used mostly by wildlife and the climbers who challenged themselves against the canyon's steep, rocky walls. He collected a backpack he had stashed in the area before he had headed to Ranger Brigade headquarters, and continued hiking, down to the bottom of the canyon, where the shallow waters of the Gunnison River roared over rocks, full to the banks with late spring snowmelt.

The river drowned out all other noise, but Dane had yet to encounter another person on this route. Once, he had surprised a black bear near the river. The animal had stood on its hind legs, neck stretched out as it sniffed him, then had dropped to all fours and bounded away. Other times, he had startled mule deer or rabbits. The deer he left alone, but he had snared more than one rabbit and roasted it over his campfire.

He followed the river for a quarter mile then turned into a narrow side canyon and began climbing. After an hour of brisk hiking, he squeezed through heavy brush, carefully placing his boots on a series of seemingly random rocks, until he emerged on a shallow rock shelf in front of a cave.

He paused and scanned the area. No footprints showed in the fine red dust he had sifted in front of the entrance to his hideaway. No one had disturbed the branches he had leaned over a portion of the opening. He sniffed the air, but detected nothing but the scent of loam. Satisfied, he slipped the pack from his back and ducked around the branches, into the opening.

He waited until he was twenty feet inside before he switched on his headlamp, the path so memorized he could have walked it with his eyes closed even though enough daylight filtered in to allow him to make out the contours of the rock walls and floor.

When he switched on the light, it illuminated a pile

of rubble—rock and dirt seemingly broken off from the walls, though he had placed it all there himself before he'd moved here. He stepped around the barrier and turned a corner into a chamber approximately eight feet square. He dropped the pack, moved to the corner and pulled a rolled sleeping bag from behind a pile of rocks, along with a duffel from which he took a bottle of water, a notebook and pen, and the last of a quail he had smoked over a fire on the riverbank the day before. He had to cook away from his hideout, to keep any hint of smoke from revealing his location.

He settled onto the sleeping bag and laid out his lunch. The cave was chilly but dry, and he felt safe here. As he ate, he opened the notebook and reviewed the contents, notes he had made about TDC, some while he was still employed there, others after he had fled to the wilderness. First were the environmental reports for the Mary Lee Mine, which showed much higher levels of radioactive isotopes than his initial assessment of the property. He could find no instances where the radioactivity of a site rose after mitigation began.

When he visited the mine to try to determine the source of this new radiation, he had suspected the material he had found there had come from some other location. At the time, he hadn't realized it was being trucked from the land TDC had donated for a new elementary school—the big scandal that had made all the papers in the wake of Ruffino's murder by one of his own bodyguards.

But that wasn't what Dane had been trying to alert

authorities to when he had passed on the conflicting environmental reports. He had expected the Ranger Brigade officers, like him, to visit the site and investigate the old mining tunnels. And that they, like him, would find the bricks of heroin and packages of fentanyl stashed there, awaiting transport to other parts of the country.

He returned to that moment in dreams sometimes— the instant where his life had changed for the worse. Other men might have realized the impact of the discovery, turned their backs on the sight and never said a word to anyone. But Dane wasn't wired that way. When he saw something wrong, he had to not only speak out but to take action to make things right.

He'd worked with men and women every day— through Welcome Home Warriors, the veterans organization he'd created—who had battled addiction to drugs. His own daughter had beat a dependence on prescription painkillers. In the past year, he had seen an uptick in addiction among the veterans he served, and he had wondered where they were getting the drugs.

Staring at the packages of carefully wrapped narcotics in the tunnels, he had known his own employer was a source. TDC was an international company with resources all over the world. In addition to shipping construction supplies and equipment across borders, it had apparently also been shipping drugs.

Donating contaminated land for an elementary school, then trying to hide the contamination, had been a petty scam, as had the illegal dumping of con-

struction debris on public land. Mitch Ruffino might
have very well come up with those ideas on his own.
Get rid of property that was a liability and look like
a philanthropist while doing so. Save a few thousand dollars on disposal fees and maybe pocket the
money himself.

But the drugs Dane had seen in that mine—
getting those drugs to Colorado had taken the coop-
eration of lots of people located in the United States
and Mexico. People who were fine with breaking the
law and destroying lives for the sake of big profits.
Underbid the competition on new construction projects as a way of building a reputation and laundering
some of the money. As far as the principals at TDC
saw it, there was no way they could lose.

Then Dane Trask had come along and tried to
ruin everything. The Ranger Brigade, and probably
his own friends and family, didn't understand why
Dane chose to live in the wilderness and operate like
a guerilla fighter rather than come forward to tell
what he knew. But TDC had the money and influence to discount anything he said. They could pay
plenty of experts to discredit him. He had imagined
how they would do it. They'd say he was suffering
from PTSD from his time in the Army Rangers. He
was delusional. They might even try to make him
out as a drug addict. He would be one man against
hundreds, and he couldn't count on law enforcement
being on his side.

But if he could steer the authorities in the right direction, so that they saw the truth and gathered the

proof themselves, then he might have a chance. The big problem now that Mitch Ruffino was gone and TDC was blaming everything on him, was getting the right people to listen. Dane had to figure out a way to get their attention—and he had to do it fast, because TDC was still hunting him, and he didn't know how much time he had before his luck ran out.

FAITH HATED AFTERNOONS like this the most—when everyone else on the team was out on patrol or working a case, leaving her and the civilian administrative assistants to answer the phone and deal with the mountains of paperwork that were part of modern law enforcement. If anything came up, she would be the officer to take the call, but in almost two months on the job, she had never had to handle anything by herself. She was capable of doing so, but she never got the chance.

When the door to the offices opened and a middle-aged man with fair skin, thinning blond hair and pale blue eyes entered, Faith perked up. The man looked around the office, a troubled expression on his face.

"May I help you?" Sylvia, one of the civilian assistants, asked.

"I'm looking for Officer Hudson," the man said.

"Officer Hudson isn't in. May I take a message?"

"Uh, I'm not sure." The man continued to look around the open office space, as if expecting to find Hud at one of the desks.

Faith rose, catching the man's eye. "Can I help you with something?" she asked.

His gaze flickered over her uniform. "Are you one of the Rangers?" he asked.

"I'm one of the officers with the Ranger Brigade, yes."

He shoved his hands into the pockets of his khakis. "It's nothing, really, just something I thought you might want to know. But maybe it isn't important."

He turned toward the door and Faith moved to intercept him. "Why don't you tell me what's on your mind? We're always happy to hear from the public." Not the complete truth—sometimes the public was annoying. But you never knew when even an annoying person might have information important to one of the cases they were working on.

The man still looked doubtful.

"I'll be sure to pass on whatever you tell me to Officer Hudson," Faith added.

He took his hands out of his pockets and nodded. "Okay."

She led him to her desk and motioned to the folding chair beside it. "I'm Officer Faith Martin," she said.

"Larry Keplar." He started to offer his hand then changed his mind and shoved it back in his pocket. He looked skittish, but sat on the edge of the chair.

"What's on your mind, Mr. Keplar?" she asked.

"I work for TDC Enterprises," he said. "I met Officer Hudson when he and another cop came to our offices to investigate a break-in a little over a week ago—before the whole mess with Mr. Ruffino."

Faith nodded, and waited. Keplar fidgeted. She

judged him to be in his late thirties or early forties, but with a boyish face. He rubbed the back of his neck. "Actually, I don't work for Terrell, Davis, and Compton anymore. I turned in my resignation this morning. I'm moving back to Kentucky, where we're from. My wife hasn't been happy here, and I got my job back with my old company. With everything going on with TDC, it felt like a good time to leave."

Faith wondered how many other employees—and customers—had decided the same thing. "What did you do at TDC?" she asked.

"I'm head of IT."

"That's a big job at a company like TDC." Flattery usually didn't hurt.

He shifted in the chair again. "That's sort of what I wanted to talk to Hud about."

"Tell me."

"I know people are saying, now that Mr. Ruffino is dead, that Dane Trask must be innocent, but I've been going through a lot of files—Trask's files. Everything from routine reports to expense accounts to, well, other stuff I found."

"What other stuff?"

She decided the best way to describe Keplar's description was "guilty." He wouldn't meet her gaze. "There were some files I don't think I was supposed to see. They were kind of hidden in the system. But you know, finding stuff like that is what I do." He shrugged.

"You found some secret files pertaining to Dane Trask?"

"Yeah. I think they might have been Trask's own files."

"What about them did you find…irregular?"

He nodded. "Irregular. That's the perfect word." He leaned toward her, more animated now. "There were reports I hadn't seen before—some of them about projects Trask never worked on, at least not officially. And expenses for two different trips to Mexico—even though he was never assigned to any jobs out of the United States. TDC has employees in Mexico to handle anything there."

"Was there something possibly illegal about these activities?" She didn't understand why Keplar had seen the need to inform the Rangers about all of this.

"Maybe. I found records that had been erased, too. I mean, it's hard to completely erase data, and I was able to restore some of it, but just fragments."

"What kind of data?"

Keplar's frown deepened the lines on his high forehead. "Shipping records. Trucking logs." He shook his head. "It doesn't make sense, but it made me wonder if Trask had been up to something illegal, after all. I mean, I know they say Mr. Ruffino was involved in some illegal stuff, but maybe he and Trask were in it together. Maybe they had a disagreement and that was why Trask left."

Faith nodded. It wasn't the most far-fetched theory she'd ever heard. "Do you have a copy of this data?" she asked.

Keplar's eyes widened. "That would be illegal. And unethical."

"Have you told anyone else about this?"

"No." He stood. "I'm not even sure I should have told you. I just thought, you know, you might want to look into it. Especially since Trask is still out there somewhere." He looked over his shoulder toward the door.

Faith rose, also. "Thank you, Mr. Keplar. We appreciate you coming in, and we'll be sure to check this out." How, she had no idea. She doubted a judge would grant a warrant to dig into TDC's "secret" records without more to support the request than this vague report.

"Yeah, well…" He wet his lips. "Nobody at TDC has to know I was here, do they? I mean, I know I've already turned in my resignation, but it wouldn't look good to future employers to know I'd been doing this kind of, um, snooping."

"I doubt it will come up. And if this does lead to something, there are laws to protect whistleblowers." At the word "whistleblower," Keplar went even paler. Without another word, he turned and fled, darting to the door and hurrying out.

Faith sat again and opened a file on her computer to summarize her interaction with Larry Keplar. As she typed, she thought about Dane Trask.

The picture of him that had been reprinted over and over in the newspaper, showed on television and featured on award posters all over town, was imprinted on her mind: a dark-haired man with intense dark eyes, chiseled cheeks, a dimpled chin, full lips and a Roman nose. Not movie-star handsome, but very masculine.

She knew he was a former Army Ranger who had spent a lot of time in the backcountry around the national park. He was reportedly fit, and smart. Tough mentally and physically—he'd have to be to have lasted almost two months living rough in the backcountry. Yes, he'd taken food from campsites a few times, but not enough to live on. He had probably stashed supplies in the area before he'd sent his truck over the rim of the canyon and made his getaway. He could hunt small game and catch the occasional fish, maybe harvest a few berries and wild greens. But it was a hard, hard way to live.

She finished typing up the statement and read through it again. The door to the office opened and second-in-command Michael Dance entered, along with Special Agent Ethan Reynolds. The men were laughing, and they brought the energy and brightness of the outdoors in with them, along with the scent of piñon. "Hey, Martin," Dance said. "Anything come up while we were out?"

Nothing I couldn't handle, she thought but said, "Larry Keplar, the soon-to-be-former head of IT at TDC Enterprises came in with a report of uncovering some secret computer files he thinks showed suspicious activity by Dane Trask. He suggested Trask and Ruffino might have been partners in TDC's illegal operations."

"What kind of files?" Ethan Reynolds, six feet tall with short brown hair and green eyes, asked.

She took a copy of her report from the printer and handed it to them. Together, they read it through and then Dance handed it back to her. "It's interesting, but pretty vague," he said. "We'll add it to the file and maybe take a closer look when Dane shows up."

"You think he's going to turn himself in?" she asked.

"Or we're going to find him," Dance said. "We're still looking, and he can't stay out there forever."

She could have pointed out that Trask had outwitted them so far, but didn't. Instead, she turned back to her computer, an idea forming in her head.

She waited until Commander Sanderlin returned about an hour later. "Sir, may I speak with you a moment?" she asked as he passed her desk. "In your office?"

"Of course." She followed him to the small corner office that had scarcely enough room for a desk, a bookcase and two visitor's chairs. She sat in one of the chairs and Sanderlin settled behind the desk. "What can I do for you?" he asked.

"I understand I was brought on to liaison with Montrose law enforcement and to serve as Public Information Officer," she said. "But neither of those occupy all my time. I'd like to expand my role."

"In what way?" Sanderlin's expression betrayed nothing.

"I want to go on patrol, take calls and investigate cases." She sat straighter. "I want to do the law enforcement work I'm trained for."

She braced herself for him to tell her she already

had a job to do, or that she didn't have enough experience or training. Instead, he sat back, the chair creaking beneath him, and fixed her with a level gaze. She looked him in the eye, refusing to be the first to blink. "Your commanding officers at the sheriff's department spoke very highly of you in their recommendations," he said. "But they suggested you would benefit from some time away from the field, in a less stressful position. I take it you don't agree."

So that's what this was all about. "I was cleared by both a medical doctor and the department's own psychiatrist for return to full duty," she said, her voice clipped as she fought to rein in her emotions. "I saw a transfer to the Ranger Brigade as an opportunity to expand my skills and prove myself in the field, and I welcomed the opportunity." She hardened her gaze and straightened her spine. "I'm not the first officer who's been taken hostage by a criminal. I survived and I've put the incident behind me." *I don't need you to protect me*, she wanted to scream. "I just want to do my job," she added. "The one I was trained for."

He nodded. "Then that's what you should do. Thank you for speaking up. And I apologize for making assumptions. I should have spoken to you about this before. As of tomorrow, you'll be part of the regular duty rotation, as your PR and liaison duties allow—though I agree, that shouldn't occupy too much of your time."

"Thank you, sir."

He nodded, and she stood and turned to leave.

"Officer Martin."

She stopped and looked back at him. "I read the report about the hostage incident," he said. "You handled yourself well, and I don't see that you were to blame for what happened. The commendation you received was well deserved."

"Thank you, sir." If he wanted to believe that, fine with her. He didn't know the whole story. Maybe no one ever would.

Chapter Three

The wildlife in the national park used the hiking trails as much as people did, so Dane made a habit of setting snares just off the trail to catch rabbit and the occasional quail or partridge. He was checking one of these snares two days after the press conference when he heard someone approaching on the trail. He eased over behind a clump of Gambel oak and waited for the hiker to pass. A single person by the sound of it—a woman or small man, moving at a deliberate pace.

Seconds later, the hiker came into view. Dane drew in a breath as he recognized Officer Faith Martin. Dressed in the khaki Ranger Brigade uniform, hiking boots, a blue daypack on her back, she scanned the area as she walked, alert. Was she searching for him? Probably, though in all the weeks he had spent both observing and eluding his pursuers, he had never seen her away from Ranger headquarters.

She was almost past him when she stiffened then stopped and slowly swiveled in his direction. He froze, heart thudding hard, and reminded himself that she couldn't see him, not even if she was looking right at him.

"Hello? Is anyone there?"

She faced him fully now, one hand on the butt of the pistol at her side. He took advantage of the proximity to study her more closely. Though slight, she looked strong, a hint of muscle in her arms and legs, though the boxy uniform and the body armor underneath hid most of her shape. She had a lovely face—heart-shaped, her sea-green eyes turned down slightly at the corners, her lashes thick and dark. He averted his gaze from those eyes, lest they somehow lock gazes as they had at the press conference, and he give himself away. Instead, he shifted his attention to her lips, which were full and pink. Feminine lips, made for sensuous kisses. Desire pulled at him, shocking in its strength.

He held his breath, reining his lust, willing his heart to slow. He reminded himself that while she might sense his presence, she wouldn't find him. Five yards of almost impenetrable underbrush separated them. By the time she hacked through all of it, he'd be long gone.

A spotted towhee sounded in the brush to his right, a high, clear call with a trill at the end. Officer Martin shifted her attention to the bird, who balanced on a high tree branch, a flash of orange and black against the dusky green of piñon. She adjusted her pack and moved on down the trail.

He should have finished checking his snares and moved away, but instead he followed, moving stealthily through the underbrush parallel to the trail, carefully placing each step. As they neared the river, the roar of its rapids drowned out everything else and he was able to move more quickly, always keeping her in sight. She intrigued him. And it made sense to try to figure out what she was up to.

She stopped at the side canyon and, after a moment's pause, left the main trail to follow a narrow animal track into the smaller canyon—the canyon where his hideout was located. To keep her in sight, he had to climb above her and move along the steep slope, struggling to place his feet carefully and not dislodge the loose rock or make noise. She studied the ground as she walked and moved slowly, picking her way along the faint trail. Was she tracking him? No—he had been very careful to cover his tracks, and most of the time avoided the game trail altogether, instead approaching the cave from a number of circuitous routes.

But she was getting too close to his hideout. Should he divert her—show himself and lead her away? His gaze shifted to the pistol at her side. He couldn't guarantee she wouldn't fire at him, but hitting a moving target on rough ground took an expert shot—and luck.

He had a gun, too, but he wouldn't use it on her. Not unless he had to defend his life.

A boulder jutted from the side of the hill, blocking his path. By the time he maneuvered around it, she was out of sight. He swore to himself. If she found his hideout, he'd have to move. He'd scouted an alternate location, but it was less convenient and not as well concealed.

More than once, he'd been tempted to turn himself in. To tell his story to the Rangers and let them go after TDC. But he couldn't guarantee they would believe him. TDC would pressure them—and the government officials who funded the task force and ultimately decided its fate. He was one man, one that TDC had spent weeks portraying as unstable and even criminal. Trusting his fate to the Ranger Brigade was a huge gamble. One he wasn't yet ready to take.

FAITH HAD ENJOYED the morning's hike, free of the confines of the headquarters building and the paperwork that threatened to swamp her desk. The opportunity to patrol on her own in the open air had her practically skipping out the door. Though the early June sun had been almost hot on the canyon rim, down here near the river was cooler, the smell of sun-warmed piñon and heated granite an energizing perfume.

She had kept her senses attuned for any sign of Dane Trask. After studying topo maps of the park, she had zeroed in on this location because the caves carved eons ago in the side canyon would make a good location for a man to hide, or even to live long-term. She had consulted Lieutenant Dance, and he'd said they had searched the area previously, but he didn't think it was a bad idea if she wanted to revisit the area. He had offered to send another officer with her, but she preferred to work alone. Maybe that didn't make her a team player, but it was the truth. Thankfully, Dance hadn't argued.

Still, she didn't hold out much hope that she'd find Trask. He was probably holed up somewhere in the backcountry, away from roads and tourists and anyone who might spot him. What was he doing out there, besides trying to find food and a place to sleep out of the weather? The few communications he'd had after he had first disappeared—cryptic notes left for his former administrative assistant and his ex-girlfriend—had indicated that he kept up with the news. But the last of those notes had appeared weeks ago. Was it possible he wasn't even alive anymore? That he had died in an accident or even by his own hand? A number of people every year chose to commit suicide in national parks.

She didn't know Dane Trask, but everything she had read about him didn't seem to point to suicide. Still, she wouldn't have said a skilled engineer, respected citizen and former soldier would have been the type to run from trouble, either. And what else was he doing out here but running away from something?

Some of her fellow deputies at the sheriff's department probably thought she was running away, too, when she had chosen to join the Ranger Brigade. No one had said anything to her face, but she had seen the way they'd looked at her, and more than one had asked a variation of "But what are you going to do there?"

She'd been tempted to tell the truth—that she

didn't care what she did in the new job, only that it offered a chance for a fresh start. She had been naïve enough to believe that her past wouldn't follow her. Of course she had assumed the commander knew her story. The whole incident had received plenty of coverage in local papers, both when it had happened and when she'd been awarded her commendation. Her fellow sheriff's deputies—the only people whose opinions really mattered to her—seemed divided between thinking she had all kinds of guts for having survived the ordeal, to believing she was stupid to have gotten herself into it in the first place.

In their shoes, she would have sided with stupid.

The biggest mistake she had made was in thinking she'd known the man who had kidnapped her. That just because she had grown up with him and knew his family, that meant she knew what he was thinking, and why he was acting the way he was.

His wife had made the 9-1-1 call on a Sunday afternoon when Faith was on duty. The wife, Liz, and Jerry Dallas were separated and when Liz had gone to pick up their four-year-old son from his usual weekend visitation with his dad, Jerry had barricaded himself in his rental house with the boy and shouted that he would shoot the kid if he didn't get what he wanted.

Faith had been one of the officers who'd responded to the scene. Because she knew him—had known him since they were nine years old and lived next door to each other—she had volunteered to talk to him. At first, it had seemed like a good move. He had listened to her, and finally invited her in to get the boy. The SWAT captain hadn't like the idea, but she had pushed for it. She knew Jerry. He wouldn't hurt her.

Except he had hurt her. The minute she'd opened the screen door to that little house, he had grabbed her by the arm, yanking her so hard she had felt the bone snap. Blinding pain had shot through her as he'd continued to pummel her, the child wailing in the background. The officers outside had said they had heard her screams.

The ordeal continued for the next thirty-six hours. If anything, her presence in the house had seemed to make things worse. Jerry had alternately raged and beat her, then threatened to kill her and the boy. She'd tried to talk to him, but he wasn't the Jerry she knew. She had realized pretty quickly that he was on drugs. Maybe meth. Maybe something else. Whatever it had been, it had fueled his rage.

He had beaten the boy, too, an adorable four-year-old named Garrett. She had tried to comfort him but, terrified and hurting, he would only rock in her arms and cry.

Then Jerry would tear him away and start punching her again.

After hours and hours of this, she had rolled under a desk to escape him and discovered a broken picture frame, probably shoved off the desk in one of his rages. The pieces of glass had cut her hand, but she had seized upon the largest jagged shard and summoned all her strength to lunge at Jerry and slash at him. As he'd clutched his bleeding face, she'd grabbed the boy and run, terrified Jerry would pursue her or that they'd both be shot by the waiting SWAT team.

Jerry did follow her out of the house, only to be cut down by the SWAT team. She and the boy were safe, though she had spent several days in the hospital and six weeks off duty, healing. When she'd returned, everyone had treated her as if she was made of glass. She'd gone through counseling and been cleared by her doctors, but a wall had gone up between her and her fellow officers. Maybe because it was such a small force and there weren't many women on it. Maybe because she had voluntarily jeopardized her safety and the safety of everyone involved by insisting on going inside that house with a man who'd already been holding one hostage.

She didn't know, but when her commander informed her the Ranger Brigade had reached out, looking for someone to handle the press and serve as a liaison, she had jumped at the chance. She'd wanted to start over someplace new. To get away from the whispers and stares.

Did the other members of the Ranger Brigade know? Probably. They read the papers and watched the news, and it had happened less than a year ago. But they didn't treat her differently because of it. She still had hope of finding a place here. Of being part of their team.

Faith had pondered all of this as she'd hiked and then something snapped her out of that dark replay of old mistakes. Suddenly, she had the eerie sense that she was being watched. The hair on the back of her neck stood up and a shiver ran down her spine. Had she spooked herself with visions of a half-wild man stalking rodents in the wilderness? She stopped to check her surroundings, but all she heard was the rush of the river and birdsong. She saw nothing but brush and rocks and the silver rapids of the river.

The feeling hadn't left her when she had turned into the narrow side canyon. She had no special reason for picking that route other than that it looked less traveled than the main trail, and should offer a view of a tributary that fed into the main channel of the river.

Rock shifted overhead and a cascade of pebbles tumbled down toward her. She froze again, holding her breath as she scanned the steep slope above. Was something up there? She thought of the stuffed mountain lion on display in the park visitor center. The big cats were said to sometimes stalk prey. She felt for the pistol at her side, reassured by its familiar shape. She wasn't the best shot on the force, but she'd scored well at the range. She had never once drawn her weapon against another person.

She continued walking, her hand hovering near the pistol, pausing to look around her every few feet. A loud "Whoop!" from below startled a cry from her, and she whirled to see a pair of fishermen on the opposite bank of the creek that formed this side canyon. A man in brown waders and a fishing vest, short white hair glinting in the sun, held up the trout he had netted while a second man, even older and more wrinkled, clapped him on the back.

Relieved, but still shaken, Faith moved down to

the water. The older man spotted her and waved then nudged the white-haired man. He held up the fish. "Just caught this beauty!" he shouted. "Biggest I ever got."

"Congratulations!" she called. She began wading toward them, picking her way on rocks, the high tops of her boots keeping her feet dry.

When she reached the other side, the two men looked worried. "It's legal to fish down here, isn't it?" the older one asked.

"I don't know," she said.

The white-haired man squinted at her. "I thought you were a park ranger. Or maybe a wildlife officer."

"Ranger Brigade," she said. "Have you see anyone else down here?"

"Not a soul," the older man said while his friend set about removing the hook from the trout. "Are you looking for someone in particular?"

"A man, forty-one years old, six foot two, with dark hair and eyes."

"Dane Trask." The white-haired man straightened. "You're looking for him, aren't you?"

"Do you know him?" she asked.

"I met him once, at a fundraiser for a veteran's group. Nice guy. Struck me as smart. I heard he'd been running around in the park, but I tend not to believe most of what I read in the papers. Why are you looking for him?"

"When people go missing in the park, we try to find them," she said. "He might be hurt and need help."

"Or maybe he just wants to be left alone." The

man bent over the fish once more. "But we haven't seen him."

"Do you come here often?" she asked.

"Our first time," the white-haired man said, wiping blood from his hands on a rag he pulled from his pocket. "It was quite the hike, but I guess it was worth it."

She nodded, and moved on. Half an hour later, the side canyon ended, choked off by cliffs and boulders the size of cars. The topo maps had showed caves in the area, but she hadn't spotted them.

She drank some water, snapped a few photos with her camera, then turned and trudged back the way she had come. The fishermen were gone now, and the feeling she was being watched had left her, as had the excitement of pursuit and the thrill of being out here on her own. Now she just felt hot and tired, and alone.

She made it back to headquarters as the sun was setting, her stomach growling with hunger and a headache pounding at her temples. The civilians had gone home for the day, as had most of the other officers. But lieutenants Dance and Knightbridge were still there, hunched over computers. They looked up when she came in. "You were out late," Randall Knightbridge said.

"Did you find anything interesting?" Dance asked.

She thought about telling him about that sensation of being watched, but dismissed the idea. "Nothing." She slid the pack from her shoulder and let it drop to the floor beside her desk, then opened the middle drawer and took out her emergency stash of dark-chocolate-covered almonds.

"You said you spoke to Larry Keplar two days ago, right?" Dance asked.

"Yes." She popped a handful of almonds into her mouth and almost groaned with pleasure.

"He seem okay to you?" Dance asked.

She swallowed and turned to him, something in his voice alerting her. "He was fine. Why?"

"They found a man dead in his car at a BLM camping area just outside the national park boundary," Knightbridge said. "The car is registered to Lawrence Keplar, so they think it might be him."

"How did he die?" she asked.

"Looks like drugs. An overdose." Dance glanced at Knightbridge.

"It might not be an accident," Knightbridge said. "We're treating it as a crime scene."

She dropped into her chair, the memory of the awkward, nervous IT man filling her mind. "Why would anyone want to murder Larry Keplar?"

"We don't know," Knightbridge said. "But maybe it was to keep him quiet."

Chapter Four

"Larry didn't do drugs. He just didn't." Jana Keplar, a woman in her forties with strong features, wore her grief like a mask, her skin gray and eyes deeply shadowed. She clenched her fists around the tissues in her hands and faced Faith and Ethan Reynolds from the sofa in the living room of a Montrose home with a For Sale sign out front. "If heroin killed him, he didn't take it voluntarily."

Reynolds had asked Faith to accompany him to the interview "because it would be good to have a woman along." It wasn't exactly a ringing endorsement of his belief in her investigative skills, but if this is what it took to be involved in the Rangers' biggest case, she would take the opportunity. "Who would want to harm your husband?" she asked.

"Dane Trask could have done it."

Reynolds and Faith exchanged surprised looks. "Why do you say that?" Reynolds asked.

"I used to work for his daughter. She fired me, but even before that, we didn't get along." Jana looked down at her lap. "He might have heard that TDC paid me to spy on her. Maybe he wanted to get back at me for that." Her lips trembled. "But he didn't have to kill Larry."

"Why did TDC want you to spy on Audra Trask?" Faith asked.

Jana sniffed, regaining her composure. "They thought she might know something about what her father had been up to." She looked at Faith again, her expression defiant. "I don't care what the media says now—Dane Trask was doing bad things. They told me he was dealing drugs—that he might have been using Audra and her school to distribute drugs to children! I had a responsibility to stop that."

"Who told you Dane Trask was dealing drugs?" Reynolds asked.

"Mr. Ruffino. Larry's boss."

"Did Larry know Mr. Ruffino paid you to spy on Audra Trask?" Reynolds asked.

"No. He…he wouldn't have liked it. Larry was a good man. Better than I deserved. Which is why I know he would never have had anything to do with drugs." She broke down, sobbing.

A woman who looked very much like Jana came in from another room. Her sister, Faith guessed. She sat and put an arm around Jana's shoulders. "Do you have to upset her like this?" she asked. "Hasn't she been through enough?"

"It will help her if we find out what really happened to her husband," Reynolds said. "Not knowing can make the loss even worse."

Jana straightened and dabbed at her eyes with the

wad of tissues. "I want you to find the person who killed Larry," she said. "I want them punished. He was a good man. He didn't deserve this."

"Your husband came to Ranger Brigade headquarters on Monday," Faith said. "He told me he was leaving TDC and you were moving back to Kentucky."

Jana nodded. "I was never happy here, and after Mr. Ruffino was killed, and the news was full of the terrible things he had done, we decided we would be better off back home. The company Larry worked for there was glad to have him back, and I was going to reopen my pre-school." She started to tear up again but fought to remain composed.

"Larry said he found some computer files that seemed odd to him," Faith continued. "Do you know anything about that?"

Jana shook her head. "No. He didn't mention anything like that to me."

"Did he bring anything home from his office? Files and things?" Reynolds asked.

"Just a few things," she said. "He hadn't been there very long."

"Could you show us what he did bring home?" Reynolds asked.

She stood and, trailed by her sister, led them into a room just off the living area. It contained a desk, a computer, a chair and a low bookcase. No pictures on the walls or books in the bookcase, as if someone hadn't finished moving in—or moving out. A banker's box sat next to the computer on the desk. "That's everything in that box," Jana said.

Reynolds lifted a large notebook from the top of the box, followed by some pictures, a couple of manuals and some other books. No flash drives or CDs or portable hard drives, or anything that might contain data. "We'll need to look at his computer," Reynolds said. "We'll send someone with a warrant to pick it up later. Please don't touch it until then."

"I won't," Jana said.

"When was the last time you saw your husband?" Reynolds asked.

She hesitated then said, "Yesterday morning."

"You didn't see him last night?" Reynolds asked.

Jana flushed. "He called about six to tell me he was going back to the office to finish up some work. We…we argued about it. I thought since he had already turned in his notice, he didn't need to be putting in overtime like that, but he insisted he had things he had to do."

"You weren't worried when he didn't come home?" Faith asked.

"Of course I was concerned. But I told myself he was annoyed we had argued and had decided to sleep at the office. He did that a few times, when he was really involved in something. I didn't like it, but there wasn't anything I could do about it. He could be very stubborn."

"Did he mention what he was working on?" Reynolds asked.

"No. He didn't really talk about his work. And if I asked, he'd tell me everything was confidential. Not that I was interested anyway."

"Other than the argument the two of you had over him working late, did your husband seem upset or worried about anything in the past few days?" Faith prompted.

"No. I'm the worrier in our marriage, not Larry. He was focused on finishing up all the projects he was involved in before we left at the end of the month, but he wasn't particularly worried."

Was that true? Faith wondered. Larry Keplar had been concerned enough about the files he had found to report it to the Ranger Brigade. Maybe Jana didn't really know her husband that well. But how many partners did? "Did he get along well with people at work?" she asked.

"I think so. Larry was a very likeable guy. That's why I can't believe someone would do this. I mean— he was harmless. The classic computer geek."

The sorrow in her eyes touched Faith. For all their differences, Jana Keplar loved her husband. "I'm sorry for your loss," Faith said. "We'll do everything we can to figure out why he died."

"Thank you," she whispered, pressing the tissues to her eyes once more.

Reynolds set his business card on the desk. "If you think of anything at all you believe might help us, please call," he said.

She nodded, and her sister moved to put her arm around her shoulders again.

Faith and Reynolds left the house. "What do you think?" Reynolds asked when they were in the Ranger SUV.

"If Larry Keplar was using drugs, his wife didn't know about it," she said. "And this is the first I've heard that Dane Trask had anything to do with drugs."

"The first I've heard, too," Reynolds said. "Is it just another way TDC is trying to discredit him, or is there something there?"

"Keplar thought Trask might have colluded with Ruffino and then they had a falling out," she said.

"Let's hope there's something on Keplar's computer that will help us figure out what was going on," Reynolds said. He glanced at her. "Why don't we take a look at where they found Keplar?"

Traffic was light on the drive from town, the late-afternoon sun glaring down, flashing on the waters of Blue Mesa Reservoir and leaching color from the rock and sagebrush along the shores. They made the turn toward the park and gradually more trees replaced the sagebrush. Visitors who thought of Colorado only in terms of the mountains were often surprised by the high desert and wide-open spaces. The road leading to the crime scene was only two miles from the national park entrance, a rutted dirt track across Bureau of Land Management property, dotted with primitive campsites. Larry Keplar's white Jeep crouched beneath a rock overhang like an animal seeking shade from the midday heat.

"One of the campers called in the report," Reynolds said. "He said he was walking his dog and realized the Jeep had been sitting there since early morning. He thought maybe someone parked it there to hike, but he walked over to investigate and saw the body slumped in the front seat. He was pretty freaked out."

"I don't blame him," Faith said. Reynolds parked the cruiser just past the corral of crime scene tape that roped off the Jeep, next to a second Ranger Brigade cruiser.

Officer Jason Beck emerged from that vehicle to greet them. "The wrecker is supposed to be here soon to haul this to our impound lot," he said.

"We just came from talking to the widow," Reynolds said. "She's pretty certain her husband wasn't an addict and that this wasn't an accident."

"The ME didn't note any obvious needle tracks," Beck said. "That was just a preliminary examination on scene. And there wasn't any other drug paraphernalia in the vehicle, not even a baggie for the heroin he used. Just the tourniquet and the needle in his arm."

Reynolds bent to peer into the car, and Faith did the same on the other side. The vehicle was cleaner than she had expected—cleaner than her own personal vehicle. No receipts or fast-food wrappers or old coffee cups, and nothing but fingerprint dust on the dash.

"Either somebody was careless about setting this up to look like an overdose, or they didn't care if we knew it was murder," Reynolds said.

"How long was the vehicle out here?" Faith asked.

"I questioned the campers who were here when I arrived," Beck said. He looked around the almost-deserted camping area. "There aren't any reservations or even formal campsites here. It's just free camping on public land, set up wherever looks good to you. Most of the people I talked to are already gone, including the guy who called it in. But everyone I spoke with said the Jeep wasn't here yesterday. One guy walked his dog about ten and said the Jeep wasn't here then. So it showed up sometime in the night."

"Keplar left Ranger headquarters about four o'clock," Faith said. "Where did he go after that?"

"Back to TDC?" Reynolds asked. "Unless he was lying when he spoke to his wife."

"Then I guess we need to verify that with TDC," Faith said.

"Good luck," Beck said.

The crunch of tires on gravel made them turn to watch an old green pickup, with splotches of primer and oversize tires, rock through ruts and around potholes toward them. The driver was a middle-aged white man in need of a shave, a grease-stained ball cap pulled down low on his forehead. When he reached them, he stopped and rolled down the window. "Something wrong, Officers?" he asked, his voice a hoarse growl.

"Have you seen this Jeep before?" Beck asked.

"It was parked here when I drove in last night." The man looked past Beck to the Jeep, festooned with crime scene tape. "And it was here when I drove out this morning. I figured someone was sleeping in it overnight."

"Are you camped around here?" Beck asked.

"Back there." The man's nod indicated further up the rutted road.

"How long have you been here?" Reynolds asked.

The man shifted his gaze to Reynolds, and past him to Faith. "A while."

BLM rules permitted camping for up to two weeks. Maybe the man had been there longer and was reluctant to admit it. Or maybe he was the type of person who stuck to a policy of saying as little as possible about his personal business to other people, particularly law enforcement.

"Did you see anyone near this vehicle either time you passed by?" Beck asked.

"Why?" the man asked. "What happened?"

"The man who owned the Jeep was found dead this afternoon," Beck said.

No change of expression. "How did he die?"

"We're not sure yet," Beck said. "Did you see anyone near the Jeep?"

"There was a guy this morning—tall guy with dark hair. He had a backpack and looked a little rough. You know, like he'd been outside a while. Homeless, or maybe just hitchhiking around." The man shrugged. "None of my business."

"What's your name?" Beck asked.

"Stacy."

"First or last name?"

"Mike Stacy."

"Could I see some identification, Mr. Stacy?" Beck asked.

Stacy frowned but then shifted and took a wallet from his back pocket. He removed a license and passed it over.

Beck made note of the information on the license and returned it to Stacy. "Did you say anything to the man you saw?" he asked.

"Nope."

"What time was this?"

"About six thirty."

"Where were you going at six thirty in the morning?" Beck asked.

"Fishing."

"Did you see anyone else in the camping area when you left?" Reynolds queried.

"No." The man shifted out of Park. "I'd better get on back to camp."

"How can we get in touch with you later if we need to talk to you?" Beck asked.

"I'll be right here," Stacy said, and drove away.

They stepped back and watched him leave. "That wasn't Larry Keplar he saw this morning," Faith said.

"No," Reynolds agreed. "But it could have been Dane Trask."

"What would Trask be doing here?" Faith asked. "And with Keplar? The two didn't even know each other."

"It would be interesting to find out," Beck said.

"It might be interesting to find out what Mr. Stacy wasn't telling us, too," Faith said.

The other two looked at her. "You think he was lying?" Reynolds asked.

"I don't think he was going fishing this morning."

"Why not?"

"I checked in the bed of the truck, and looked

through the window. No cooler. No fishing pole or tackle box."

"Maybe he has everything neatly tucked away," Beck said.

"Maybe." Or maybe he had been doing something else he didn't want cops to know about. He could have been visiting his mistress or robbing a convenience store or working under the table for a construction company. It probably didn't have anything to do with their case, but Faith hated loose ends.

"After the wrecker hauls away Keplar's Jeep, I'll talk to Stacy again," Beck said.

"Want us to back you up?" Reynolds asked.

Beck shook his head. "Anyway, the wrecker's here."

The three of them turned to watch a wrecker rumble up the rutted road. "We're going to head back to headquarters to see if the ME's report has come in," Reynolds said.

"See you there," Beck returned.

Faith's phone rang as they were pulling up to the entrance to the national park. "We need you here at the office," Dance said. "Someone at the ME's office leaked news of Larry Keplar's death and we're getting a lot of calls from the press."

"I'm just a couple of minutes away," she said.

"I heard," Reynolds said as she pocketed her phone. "I'm curious to know what was leaked, to get the media so excited."

Dance greeted them as they entered the building. "Briefing in the conference room in two," he said.

"I've got the admins issuing 'no comment' statements until you can take over, Martin."

All the officers on duty convened in the conference room, where Commander Sanderlin stood at the head of the table. "We have the ME's preliminary report on Larry Keplar's body," he said. "We don't know who in their office leaked the information to the press, but our policy is not to confirm or deny the information." He looked to Faith.

"We cannot comment on an ongoing investigation," she said.

Sanderlin nodded. "As for the report itself, it shows the cause of death as an overdose of a mixture of heroin and fentanyl. No evidence of previous opioid use, so we're treating this as a suspicious death, possibly murder."

He looked to Reynolds. "Did you and Martin learn anything from Keplar's widow?"

"He contacted her about an hour after he left here Monday," Reynolds said. "He told her he was going back to work at TDC. When he didn't come home, she assumed he spent the night at the office. Apparently, he did that sometimes. We'll be contacting TDC to verify that."

Sanderlin consulted the notes on a tablet before him. He was about to speak when a knock on the door interrupted him. "Come in," he called.

Sylvia entered. "I have that report you've been waiting on," she said.

Sanderlin took the paper she offered and glanced at it. His frown deepened. He waited until the door closed behind Sylvia before he spoke. "This is a preliminary report on the evidence we collected from Keplar's Jeep," he said. He looked up, his expression grave. "Fingerprints on the driver's-side door are a match for Dane Trask."

Chapter Five

Dane straddled the thick branch of a lodgepole pine and settled back against the trunk, making himself comfortable as he watched the group around the white Jeep. The female Ranger Brigade officer, Faith Martin, was there with two men who also wore the Ranger Brigade uniform. How was it that he had never seen the woman before Monday and lately he'd run into her at every turn? She was speaking now, and he wished he knew what she was saying. She looked intense. Like she was focused on the job.

They were talking about the Jeep, probably. Or more likely, the dead man who had been inside the vehicle. Dane didn't know who the man was, though he had been white, clean-cut, with no sign of camping gear. Dane had noticed the Jeep early this morning when he'd come to this place to meet up with a friend. Steve Betcher was a fellow Army Ranger Dane had reconnected with after they'd both been discharged. After Dane had disappeared into the park, Betcher had started hanging around the camping area where Dane had been taking food from campers. He'd started leaving things out for Dane, along with notes that he wanted to help.

Betcher had promised to never betray Dane, and Dane knew Steve's word was gold. So now they met every ten days or so at this BLM camping area. It felt safer than the park. Most of the people who came here kept to themselves and minded their own business. Some of them were vacationers who liked free camping, while others were perpetual travelers on a tight budget, or the homeless looking for somewhere to sleep where they wouldn't be hassled.

The news from Betcher this time was full of the death of TDC vice president Mitch Ruffino and the revelations that he had tried to pass off a hazardous waste site as safe enough for an elementary school, and other crimes, including possible murder. TDC was claiming to have had no knowledge of Ruffino's crimes and running a campaign of public appearances, generous donations and extensive PR to rebuild their reputation.

"Money talks," Betcher had said. "And they're throwing plenty of it around. People are saying TDC couldn't have known what Ruffino was up to."

"I'll never believe that," Dane had said.

"Then why not come forward and say so?" Betcher had asked.

"Because it isn't safe. For me or for others." It was the answer Dane had given every time Betcher asked, but he was beginning to question whether it was the right answer. Did he have enough evidence to persuade the right people—law enforcement and government officials—that TDC's construction empire was just a front for their drug smuggling and distribution business?

After he'd collected the food and newspapers Betcher brought him, Dane had circled back to the Jeep to check it out. Something about the vehicle had struck him as wrong. He had seen the man inside and tried the door. It was locked. He'd looked closer and seen the tourniquet and the needle. Was this an addict who'd come to the camping area to shoot up? If so, his drugs had probably been supplied by TDC Enterprises.

Instead of moving on, Dane had climbed this tree and kept watch over the Jeep. Eventually, a camper had discovered the dead man, and law enforcement had descended. The body of the man had been taken away, crime scene tape strung and evidence gathered. Officer Martin and her two male companions were the latest arrivals to view the scene. Dane wondered what they had concluded.

His attention returned time and again to the woman. If he told her what he knew, would she believe him? Would she help him? He had been trained to fight back, to take care of himself under extreme circumstances. But TDC felt too big for one man to take on alone. He was doing what he could, operating like a guerrilla fighter. But he wasn't doing enough. Maybe Betcher was right and it was time to ask for help.

An old pickup rolled into view and the driver stopped to talk to the officers. From his perch in the tree, Dane could see nothing of the driver and couldn't overhear the conversation, but it wasn't hard to imagine the discussion. The man, curious, would ask what was going on. The officers, always on the lookout for evidence, would try to determine what the man knew. After a few moments, the man rolled on. He was probably a camper. There were half a dozen scattered over the roughly two acres of BLM property that bordered the national park, offering a no-frills, budget-minded alternative to the reserved campsites within the park itself.

Dane waited a little while longer, the sun filtering through the pine needles and warming his face, the scent of pine enveloping him. He'd certainly had worse surveillance positions. A wrecker arrived. Martin and the man she had arrived with left. The Jeep was hauled away and the other officer also left. Time for Dane to return to the park, read the papers Betcher had brought, and plan his next move.

He followed an old animal trail that skirted the campground toward the park boundary. He moved swiftly but silently, carefully planting his feet and alert for any indication that he was being followed. But he hadn't expected trouble to come from ahead of him. When the man in the ball cap stepped out in front of him, a hefty pistol steadied in both hands, Dane froze.

"Keep your hands where I can see them, Trask," the man ordered, his voice hoarse and harsh.

Dane kept his hands out to his sides and studied the man. He was big, but the bigness was muscle, not fat. He wore loose jeans, an untucked, button-down chambray shirt and the ball cap. Clothes that would help conceal a weapon and be easy to move in. Clothes that would make a lot of people overlook him.

"What are you doing here?" Dane asked.

"I've been waiting for you." The man gestured with the pistol. "Throw out your weapon."

Dane didn't move. The man took a step closer. Something about the way he moved—and the fact that he had found Dane here, on this faint trail on the edge of the park—made him think this wasn't another of the countless amateurs who had descended on the park in the hope of collecting the ridiculously large reward TDC had offered for Dane's capture. This man knew how to handle himself, which meant he was either law enforcement, military—or a professional who operated on the wrong side of the law.

"Throw the gun out here or I will shoot," the man said, taking another step closer.

Dane eased the pistol out of the holster at his back and dropped it into the pine needles beside the trail. "Who sent you?" he asked.

"Who do you think?" The man gestured with the pistol again. "Turn around."

"Why? So you can shoot me in the back?"

That earned him a clout on the side of the head that made his ears ring. But it told him the man with the gun didn't want to fire it if he didn't have to. Gunfire, so near other people, might draw the wrong kind of attention. "What were you doing just now, watching the Rangers?" the man asked.

"I wanted to see what they were doing." Now he knew the man had training. The average person rarely looked up for anything. Had he been the man in the pickup who'd stopped to talk to the Rangers?

"You say one word to them and you and your daughter are dead," the man said. Then he made as if to hit Dane with the pistol again.

Dane dodged the blow, dropped to the ground and kicked his assailant hard in the shin. The man let out a grunt and stumbled. Dane came up hard, hitting the man under the chin with his head and then jumping back and aiming a savage kick at the man's wrist. Before the guy could recover from one blow, Dane hit him again. His assailant dropped the gun and began swinging his fists, but Dane was relentless. He either dodged or ignored the man's attacks, pummeling him until he lay in a heap on the ground, moaning.

Breathing hard, blood running down the side of his face from where he had been pistol-whipped, and his lip swollen from another blow, Dane searched in the pine needles until he found both weapons. He pocketed both, then jogged away, fear and adrenaline propelling him forward. He had been closer to death now than he had at any time in this whole dangerous game.

How much longer could he fight and keep winning?

"ARE DANE TRASK'S prints anywhere else in Larry Keplar's Jeep? Or on the syringe?" Faith's question interrupted a lively discussion about how Trask's prints had ended up on the door of Keplar's Jeep.

Commander Sanderlin shook his head. "The inside of the Jeep, along with the drug paraphernalia, showed no prints—not even Keplar's."

"Someone wiped it clean," Reynolds said.

"Why go to all the trouble to clean the inside of the Jeep and not bother with the door?" Faith asked.

"Someone was coming and he was in a hurry to leave?" Dance suggested.

"Or maybe Dane's prints are unrelated to Keplar's death," Reynolds said. "Maybe he was hitchhiking and Keplar gave him a ride."

"In that case, the prints would be on the passenger door," Officer Mark Hudson pointed out.

"The report notes that Trask's were the only prints found on the door," Sanderlin said. "The door was actually much cleaner around the handle than anywhere else, indicating it was wiped."

"Then Trask could have come along after the killer left," Faith said. "Maybe he saw the car and was looking in. That goes along with what our witness said about seeing Trask next to the car."

"Then why didn't he report Keplar's death?" Hud asked.

"No access to a phone?" Faith suggested. "Or he was worried about getting caught."

"We can't rule him out as a suspect," Sanderlin said. "Did Trask have a motive for murdering Keplar?"

"Keplar said he didn't know Trask—the two never met," Dance said.

"So why would Trask kill the man?" Faith asked.

"Keplar said he had come across files he thought showed Trask had been up to something suspicious," Reynolds noted. "Did Trask kill Keplar to keep him from revealing what was in those files?"

"Do you think Trask wiped down the door of the Jeep, then came back later and left his prints there?" Faith asked.

"It's possible," Reynolds said. "Mike Stacy said he saw a man who looked like Trask by the Jeep when he left this morning."

"Killing someone with a heroin overdose takes planning," Commander Sanderlin said. "While it's possible Trask was carrying drug paraphernalia with him all these weeks, we haven't found anything in his past to indicate drug usage."

"Maybe Trask saw who killed Larry Keplar and tried to help him," Hud offered.

"We have a lot of theories and no clear proof of any of them," Dance said.

"Go back to the scene and interview the campers again," Sanderlin said. "Maybe someone else saw something or heard something. And, Martin?"

She froze in the act of sliding back her chair. "Yes, sir?"

"You deal with the press. Come up with a bare-bones statement that sticks to the facts but doesn't reveal anything that would jeopardize our investigation."

"Yes, sir." That was why she had been hired, after all—to free up the more experienced investigators to do their job. For now, at least, she was back on the sidelines.

The sun was setting by the time Faith answered the last phone call and issued the last statement. The forensics experts combing through Keplar's Jeep hadn't come up with anything significant, and the only thing Reynolds's and Beck's return to the campsite had revealed was that Mike Stacy had left and no one else appeared to have seen or spoken to the man. The tags on his vehicle were registered to a Wendell Stacy, at an address in Ohio different from the one on the license Beck had copied. No one had been able to make contact with Wendell, but they'd try again tomorrow. Nobody was holding out much hope Mike would be of any help to them—he was just another loose end that needed tying up.

She made her way to her green Subaru Forester at the far end of the lot, pausing to wave to Officer Knightbridge as he drove past on his way out, his canine partner, Lotte, with her nose out the window of the backseat. Faith was really looking forward to getting home, taking off this uniform, and enjoying a glass of wine and an episode or two of the British dramas that were her guilty pleasure. Dane Trask and his stupid games of hide-and-seek could wait until another day.

She hit the button on her key fob to unlock the car doors and started to slip her purse from her shoulder when a hand clamped over her mouth and a strong arm encircled her chest and lifted her off the ground. "I'm not going to hurt you," a voice growled in her ear. "But you have to come with me."

Chapter Six

Every instinct told Faith to fight back against the man who held her. She squirmed and kicked, connecting once with his kneecap, which made him swear, but he didn't loosen his hold on her. He was strong, and a lot bigger than she was. And someone, somewhere, had taught him how to gain the upper hand in a struggle. Within seconds he had slapped a piece of tape over her mouth, tied her hands and feet and slung her over his shoulder in a fireman's carry. Then he was running, feet pounding on a dirt trail that ran adjacent to the road, behind the closed park visitor center, and into the canyon.

In the fading darkness, Faith tried to make note of the direction they headed. Bound as she was, she could no longer fight her captor, for fear of falling and breaking bones or, worse, hitting her head on one of the many rocks scattered on either side of the trail.

Her captor slowed from a jog to a brisk walk. He was breathing hard, but he still held her firmly. Faith tried to make noise, to call out, but only achieved a pathetic whimper. "You're going to be okay," the man said. "I won't hurt you."

She didn't believe the words. Jerry had said that at first, too. And he had been someone she'd considered a friend. She still bore scars from the beatings he had given her, emotional as well and physical. As this stranger carried her farther into the darkness, her heart pounded and it took all her effort to fight waves of panic. Her arms ached from her constant straining against the ligatures, and her neck and shoulders throbbed from her efforts to hold up her head to try to see where they were going.

They moved deeper into the canyon, and the sound of running water drowned out even the pounding of her heart. Her captor didn't slow his steps, even though he must be exhausted. She wasn't a big woman, but carrying a little more than a hundred and twenty pounds over such a long distance would have been impressive, under other circumstances.

At some point in their struggle, he had disarmed her. She'd lost her purse, too, and her keys. She hoped she had dropped them by the car. Someone would see them and realize something had happened to her. Except that everyone else on the team had left ahead of her, as had the park rangers. It might be morning before anyone thought to investigate why her car was still parked in the lot.

They were climbing again, the man breathing hard once more. Then he stopped and lowered her to the ground. She glared up at him, though she could see little in the darkness, just a general impression of a tall, muscular man with long hair and a beard. "I'm going to carry you inside," he said. "Once there, I'll uncover your mouth and I'll untie your hands. Don't try to fight or try to escape. I don't want to hurt you, but I will keep you here until you've heard me out."

Faith could say nothing. She could do nothing but groan as he gathered her in his arms; not slung over his shoulder now, but cradled by strong arms and hands that were surprisingly gentle. She turned her face away from him, but his scent surrounded her— clean male sweat and woodsmoke. It wasn't an unpleasant aroma, but one that added to her fright. She now had an idea who had captured her.

He carried her deep into a cave and set her gently against the wall. "This is going to sting," he said then slid his thumbnail under one corner of the tape over her mouth and tugged hard.

"Owww!" she protested, tears stinging her eyes.

He switched on a lamp, a battery-operated lantern that cast a bright white glow across the low-ceilinged chamber. Faith stared up at the man. "What do you want with me, Dane Trask?"

DANE LOWERED HIMSELF to the floor across from Faith. It didn't surprise him she knew who he was—the Rangers had been looking for him for weeks. "I don't want to hurt you," he said. "But I need your help."

Fury sparked her eyes, which looked black in the dim light, though he knew them to be green. "Did you think of just asking? You know 'Hello, Officer. I need your help.'"

"My life is in danger," he said. "And the life of my daughter. I can't risk exposing myself."

"But you'd risk kidnapping a law enforcement officer?" Her anger hadn't dimmed one bit. Her fingers curled at her sides, like claws. He had no doubt if he came close to her, she'd lash out at him.

"I'm not kidnapping you."

"You took me by force, against my will. How is that not kidnapping?"

He grimaced. "I can see how you might think of it that way, but I needed to get your attention, and to take you someplace safe, where we could talk." She wasn't buying it—and he couldn't say he blamed her. Had his impulsiveness once again led him to the wrong choice?

"You need to let me go," she said.

"I can untie your ankles," he said. "I can even let you walk out of here. But it's full dark out there now. You don't know where you are, and it isn't safe."

"I'm not an idiot," she said. "I'm a trained law enforcement officer."

"Have you been trained in wilderness survival?" he asked. "Do you know how to navigate without a map in the dark? Are you going to risk climbing out of the canyon on an unmarked trail with very little light? You could easily fall and be injured, if not killed. And that's not even taking into account the wild animals that are out there."

Fear flickered across her face, but she hardened her expression against it. "All I have to do is get away from you and wait until daylight," she said.

"Or you could stay here, where you'll be safe and warm and dry and fed. And all I ask is that you listen to what I have to say. In the morning, I'll take you back to the trail up to the visitor center."

"You need to return my weapon."

"In the morning." She was angry enough with him now she might try to shoot him. She would probably at least try to arrest him. He didn't want to have to fight her again. "I'm not going to hurt you." Maybe if he repeated the words enough, she'd believe him.

She stared at him a long time without saying anything. He waited. As impulsive as he could be sometimes—not always to good results—when he put his mind to it, he could be very patient. "Untie my ankles," she said finally.

Did that mean she was going to stay and listen? He decided to risk it. He took out his pocketknife and, holding it so he could defend himself if necessary, approached her. He squatted at her ankles and sliced through the tape that bound her. She tried to lurch up, and cried out, as he had known she would.

He retreated to his sleeping bag across from her. "Wait for the circulation to return," he said. Watching her out of the corner of his eye, he took a thermos from his pack, filled a cup and slid it across the floor of the cave toward her. "It's tea," he said, and filled the thermos cap for himself. Then he took the container of fried chicken Betcher had delivered that morning and slid it toward her. "Eat something. You'll feel better." He added rolls and fruit to the spread, and began to eat.

She stared at the food as if it was booby-trapped. "What camper did you steal this from?" she asked.

"I never stole." Every time he had taken food, in the early days before Betcher had reached out to him, he had left behind something of value, often an item worth far more than the few things he'd taken. "And this didn't come from a camper."

She studied the label on the chicken, which was from a local supermarket, then, still watching him, helped herself to a piece.

She ate carefully, with delicate movements, still tensed, watching him. She kept shifting on the hard stone. "Here." He pulled a blanket from behind him and tossed it to her. "Sit on this. It will be more comfortable."

She wanted to argue, he could tell, but she had sense enough not to. She folded the blanket neatly then sat on it and continued eating. She didn't speak until she had picked the chicken clean and finished her tea. "You're supposed to be a very smart man," she said, her voice even. "But you're not behaving very smart right now."

He bowed his head, accepting her assessment. "That should tell you how desperate I am," he said. Desperate to survive, and desperate for someone—especially for this woman—to believe him.

FAITH WASN'T HUNGRY ANYMORE, but she forced herself to eat. She may not have had wilderness survival training, but she knew enough to not pass up a meal.

She would need all her strength and a clear head to escape this man.

Though she couldn't see him clearly from where he sat in the shadows, she could feel his gaze on her. Studying her, the way he must have studied her before, to plan taking her. Just as he must have scoped out this hideout before he'd sent his pickup crashing into the canyon and left behind the life he had known. She hadn't been able to make out much on the journey here, but they hadn't traveled more than an hour from Ranger headquarters, which meant this hideout was only two or three miles off the park's main road. Yet the dozens of people, maybe even hundreds, who had searched for him had never found him.

That led her to the question of food. The date on the chicken package was today, and it certainly tasted fresh. Did he have a vehicle stashed somewhere and a disguise that allowed him to make the thirty-mile trek to Montrose for supplies? That seemed improbable.

That meant he had someone outside the park who was helping him. But who? His daughter seemed a likely choice, but she and Officer Mark Hudson were practically living together. And in every interaction Faith had had with Audra, she'd come across as truly worried about her dad and eager to cooperate in any way with the people searching for him.

"Are you ready to listen to my story?" he asked.

Yes, she wanted to hear whatever tale he would decide to spin for her. Even more important, the longer he talked, the longer she had to figure a way out of her predicament. "If you expect me to listen to you, then you owe me the courtesy of moving to where I can see your face and hands." She needed to know what he was up to.

He scooted forward, until the lamp cast a harsh white light across his face. Even beneath the beard, it was a face familiar to her from his file at Ranger headquarters, and from the reward posters plastered all over town. Yet she could understand how someone who wasn't trained to notice and remember faces might not connect the man before her with the handsome, clean-cut image on those posters. The man in front of her had shaggy hair, heavily streaked with gray, and a roughly trimmed beard. One side of his lip was swollen and his cheek was bruised, as if he'd recently been in a fight.

As Faith studied him more closely, he met her assessing gaze with a look of challenge—an expression that touched something inside her, calling forth heat and something like longing. With a jolt, she realized where she had experienced a similar gaze. "You were at the press conference Monday," she said. "The man in the bandana."

"I wanted to hear what excuses TDC would make this time," he said. "But then I saw you there and thought you might be the one who could help me."

How did I get so lucky? she thought, rueful. "Why me?" Was it because she was young and therefore, to his mind, gullible? Or because she was a woman, more susceptible to a good-looking man?

"I'd seen your name in the papers," he said. "You're the media liaison, so you have contacts with local reporters, which could be useful. And you're a local, not an outsider, like so many of the others. That makes the crimes TDC is committing more personal."

"A crime doesn't have to be personal for a good law enforcement officer to want justice," she said.

"No. But I'm taking a big risk," he said. "I need the odds stacked in my favor as much as possible."

"What crimes are you referring to?" she asked. "Do you mean building a school on property TDC knew was contaminated? Or the illegal dumping on federal land? Or the murder of Roy Holliday?" The Rangers were pretty sure Mitch Ruffino was behind the murder of the reporter, whose body had been found at the same illegal dump site TDC had used to dispose of hazardous materials.

"I think Roy Holliday was killed because he figured out what was really going on," Dane said. "What happened to him would have happened to me if I hadn't left when I had."

She shifted, the blanket he had provided offering limited protection from the hard ground. "I'm listening."

THROUGH LONG, SLEEPLESS nights in this cave, Dane had planned how he would present his case. He began with the bare facts: his discovery of the discrepancies between his initial assessment of the Mary Lee Mine over a year ago and tests taken by others three months ago, then his visit to the mine and his discovery of bricks of heroin in the mine tunnel.

"Men and women I worked with at Welcome Home

Warriors told me heroin was easy to get and relatively cheap," he said. "They claimed high-quality product came up from Mexico in regular shipments. I wondered what the connection was between what I'd seen at the mine and those shipments. So I started digging deeper. I discovered that in the previous two years, TDC had greatly expanded its business in Mexico. After the disaster with the Chinese drywall, they turned to a supplier in Mexico City, and truck after truck loaded with building materials crossed the border and made its way to Montrose."

"Buying products in Mexico isn't illegal," Faith said.

"No. But I decided to go to Mexico myself. I was planning a vacation there when TDC assigned me to do an assessment for a new property they had just acquired—a former factory they planned to convert to loft apartments." He leaned closer, wanting to see her more clearly, to make sure she understood his explanation. "It's the kind of project that can be a real moneymaker, as long as there aren't problems like asbestos or contaminated groundwater, or other hazards. So I went down there, and while I was there, I took a day and visited the drywall factory. I followed the trucks and I saw that some of them took a slightly different route to the border, stopping overnight in the countryside. While the driver slept, other men added additional cargo to panels underneath the trucks."

"Border Patrol screens for those things," Faith said.

"Occasionally, they catch a single shipment," Dane said. "But the truck driver is a contractor. He doesn't work for TDC. TDC blames him, and, if necessary, they bribe the right people. No one has ever accused TDC of anything but being the occasional victim of a corrupt contractor."

"What happens after the drugs get to Colorado?" she asked.

"The driver parks the truck at a TDC warehouse and spends the night at a nearby motel while the truck is unloaded. TDC workers remove the legitimate cargo of drywall, but that night, one or two other people unload the narcotics. It's a remote location, with no cameras and no one else to notice anything irregular."

"But you noticed."

"Because I went looking. I spent three nights in a row watching and filming."

She leaned toward him. "Where are the films?"

"Someplace safe, if TDC hasn't found them and destroyed them."

"You need to turn them over to the Ranger Brigade."

"I'll give them to you," he said. "If you believe me."

She met his gaze, her expression unreadable. There was skepticism there, even outright dislike. But some warmer emotion, too, as if part of her did believe he was telling the truth, or at least, wanted to believe.

FAITH STUDIED DANE TRASK, who was every bit the wild man she had begun to picture, yet much more complex. He didn't strike her as a man in the grip of a delusion, but what he was suggesting sounded far-fetched. "Why would a legitimate business like TDC Enterprises get involved in drug dealing?" she asked. "It's incredibly risky. In addition to being illegal and dangerous, there's the not inconsiderable challenge of laundering the money you make, and the problem of concealing the illegal activities—which, according to you, they've been able to hide for a long time."

"Construction is a business that's very sensitive to economic ups and downs," he said. "It's also highly regulated, at least the types of big projects that TDC handles. Profit margins can be very slim, and bad business decisions can have a big impact on the bottom line." Was he giving her too much detail? But this was all important. He forged on. "Two years ago, TDC was on the verge of bankruptcy. An office complex they were building in China burned down and they lost a great deal of money. They were caught in that scandal over toxic drywall from China. They had to reimburse several big clients and they faced lawsuits from others. They needed a big infusion of cash. Somehow, they hit upon dealing drugs as the answer. With projects all over the world and trucks regularly transporting materials across borders, plus their stellar reputation, they were ideally situated to succeed. And they kept up with their legitimate projects as a perfect way to launder the profits from the drugs. As for keeping their activities secret, the kind of money they're making can buy a lot of silence."

"I don't understand how the school and the Mary Lee Mine tie into this," she said.

"They don't, except that they were using the mine tunnels as an out-of-the-way place to store some of their drug shipments. I think once they started down a corrupt path, it got easier to take other shortcuts. Someone—maybe Mitch Ruffino, maybe someone above him—saw the opportunity to get rid of that piece of land, which wasn't good for anything, by donating it for the school. They thought they could get away with trucking the contaminated material from the school construction site to the mine the federal government was paying them to mitigate and no one would be the wiser."

"But you figured out what was going on," she said. "Why didn't anyone else see it?"

"The simplest answer is that they weren't looking. And TDC was clever enough to make sure that different people filed the different reports showing contaminate levels. They didn't count on me double-checking my own work and noticing the discrepancies."

"All right. Let's assume everything you say is true. Why not bring this to the police right away?"

"I'm pretty sure at least some of the local cops receive regular 'donations' from TDC."

"You could have gone to the FBI. Or the Ranger Brigade. I can promise you, TDC isn't paying us off."

He nodded. "I probably should have done that."

"So why didn't you?"

He looked away. "All my adult life, my first approach when I see a problem is to figure out how to solve it. Myself."

She stared at him, letting the words sink in. "You

thought you were going to stop an international drug operation by yourself?"

"Obviously, I didn't think it through."

"Obviously. What did you do?"

"I confronted Mitch Ruffino with the evidence I had collected. First, he tried to deny it. Then he offered me a bribe. When that didn't work, he had a couple of guys come to my house and try to kill me. When they didn't succeed, he sent pictures of my daughter—pictures proving they had been in her house and had her under surveillance. He told me as long as I kept quiet, Audra would live."

"You definitely should have gone to the police then."

"I still didn't know who I could trust. And those pictures of Audra—they shook me. I thought the best thing for me to do was to disappear. I tried to leave hints, to get people to look closer at the mine, so they'd find the drugs I'd seen. But by the time anyone figured it out, TDC must have moved the stash."

"Why didn't you just tell us what was going on?" Honestly, she wanted to shake the man.

"I didn't want the information to come from me," he said. "If someone else figured it out, that would take the heat off of Audra."

"But no one else did figure it out, so you decided kidnapping me was the solution to everything." She didn't try to keep the disdain from her voice.

"They killed that man in the Jeep at the BLM camping area," he said. "Then they sent someone else after me. I feel like I'm running out of time to stop them."

"What do you know about the man in the Jeep?"

"I've never seen him before, but he had a TDC parking sticker on his Jeep. I saw the needle in his arm and figured he died of an overdose. Whether he did it himself or someone did it to him, I blame TDC. Who was he?"

She hesitated then said, "His name was Larry Keplar. He was head of IT for TDC, hired just after you left. He came to Ranger headquarters on Monday afternoon to tell me he had come across some files that showed you were up to no good. He thought you and Mitch Ruffino were working together to defraud taxpayers and endanger schoolchildren."

Dane frowned. "I was definitely not working with Ruffino. This Keplar must have seen some of the discrepancies I noticed when I started digging, and reached the wrong conclusion."

Was he telling the truth? She wanted to believe him, partly because doing so would help wrap up this whole messy case. But Dane Trask had plenty of reasons to lie to protect himself and win her trust. "It doesn't matter if I believe you or not," she said. "What counts is the evidence, and what it shows."

"I have evidence," he said. "But TDC will have worked to move things around and hide their activities even more. I'll need help to uncover everything."

"Investigating these allegations will be our job," she said.

"That's why it's important that you believe me,"

he said. "And it's another reason I turned to you for help."

"I don't understand," she said, unnerved by the intensity of his gaze, like a physical caress.

"Your name," he said. "Faith. I need you to have faith that I'm telling the truth."

He was asking her to trust him. After he'd tied her up and hauled her off to his hiding place like some caveman stealing a bride from an enemy tribe? A shiver raced up her spine at the idea. But it wasn't a shiver of fear, more of…anticipation. As if some part of her she was fighting to deny wanted to stay there with him to see what happened next.

Chapter Seven

"Faith Martin is missing."

Commander Sanderlin faced the officers and civilian support staff who crowded the conference room Thursday morning, filling every chair around the long table and lining the walls. Carmen Redhorse studied the faces of her fellow officers, each one grave with concern.

"She was apparently taken yesterday evening, after she unlocked her vehicle but before she could get in," Sanderlin continued. "Lieutenant Dance spotted her purse and her keys lying on the gravel next to her Subaru when he arrived this morning."

"I came in early to catch up on some reports," Dance said. "I was surprised to see Martin's car out there, since I know she worked late last night. When she wasn't in the office, I went out to check, thinking she might have had car trouble and caught a ride with someone else. The purse was dumped on the ground by the driver's-side door, the keys a short distance away. No scuff marks or any sign of a struggle."

"I waved goodbye when I drove out of here last

night," Knightbridge said. "Martin was walking to her car and she looked fine. There wasn't anyone else in the parking lot."

"They could have driven up after you left," Dance said.

"Do you know if she has a significant other or family in town?" Carmen asked.

The question was met with blank stares. Carmen felt a stab of guilt. Faith Martin was such a recent addition to the team, none of them knew much about her. Truth be told, they hadn't really tried to get close to her. She was the public information officer. A desk cop. Not really "one of them." And she was a young woman, which made it even tougher. Carmen, the only other female on the team, should have done more to include her.

"She never talked about her personal life," Mark Hudson said.

"I spoke with her former supervisor at the sheriff's office," Sanderlin said. "He said he would ask among her friends in the department. They want to be a part of our search efforts."

"Who would take her right out of the parking lot?" Knightbridge asked. "And why?"

"Someone targeting her personally?" Hud asked. "Her name is in the paper as the Ranger Brigade spokesperson. Has she received any threats?"

"None that she reported," Sanderlin said. "Though I want you to go through her computer to see what you find."

"It could have been someone with a grudge against

cops," Knightbridge pointed out. "She was wearing her uniform."

"She's a woman," Carmen said. "Sometimes, that's all it takes to be a target."

Nods from the other women in the room; uncomfortable silence from the men.

"There was a biker at the press conference on Monday," Carmen said. "He was watching her pretty intently."

"Who was he?" Hud asked.

Carmen shook her head. "I've never seen him before, and I don't think he spoke to Faith, or even came very close. But he definitely noticed her."

"We'll try to find him," Sanderlin said. "Anything else?"

"Maybe Dane Trask kidnapped her," Ethan Reynolds said.

"Why do you suggest that?" Sanderlin asked.

"He seems to be connected with a lot of irregular, if not outright illegal, activities in and around the park since he began hiding out here," Reynolds commented. "He's frustrated all our efforts to apprehend him. Maybe Martin spotted him and he kidnapped her to keep her from revealing his whereabouts."

"He might even have known she was kidnapped before and been inspired to act," Knightbridge said.

So, Carmen wasn't the only one who remembered that Faith Martin had been taken hostage in a standoff with a man less than a year ago. Whether out of a reluctance to pry or an inclination to avoid embarrassing her, none of them had ever mentioned it before now. "To this point, Trask has acted with a purpose," she said. "His motivations don't always seem logical to us, but he does appear to have a reason for everything he has done. What reason would he have to kidnap Faith?"

"If she discovered his hideout, he would need to protect that," Reynolds said.

"His hideout isn't visible from our parking lot," Carmen said. "And if Faith knew where he was hiding before she headed to her car last night, I don't think she would have kept that information to herself."

"Kidnappers usually have an objective in mind," Sanderlin said. "A list of demands, or someone they want to exchange their hostage for. We haven't had any communication of that sort regarding Martin."

And some people killed just to be killing, Carmen thought, but she didn't voice the idea out loud. She didn't have to. Every officer in this room had worked or heard about cases where someone died simply because they were in the wrong place at the wrong time.

"I don't think we're getting anywhere with this discussion," Sanderlin said. He turned to Knightbridge. "Take Lotte and see if you can trail Martin and whoever took her. Hud, you look through her computer files. Carmen, you and Reynolds talk to park rangers, then interview campers in the park. Maybe one of them was coming or going at that hour and saw something. Then work with Hud to try to identify the biker you saw at the press conference."

"Right." Carmen pushed back her chair.

When she and Reynolds left Ranger headquarters,

Knightbridge and his Belgian Malinois search dog, Lotte, were circling Martin's green Subaru Forester.

"What do you think the odds are that a woman would end up kidnapped twice in one year?" Reynolds asked.

"They're probably higher for a cop than most people," Carmen said.

"I don't know a single other law enforcement officer who's been in that situation," Reynolds said.

"I knew a DEA agent who was held hostage by a drug supplier," she said. "And a prison guard inmates used to help them escape."

"Okay, so it happens. Just not that often. Not twice in one year to the same person."

"People get struck by lightning twice more than you might think," she said. "I really don't care about the statistics. I just want to find her before she's hurt."

"I want to find her, too," Reynolds said. "But it would help if we knew why someone wanted her in the first place."

The rangers on duty at the park visitor center expressed concern over Martin's disappearance, but none of them had seen anyone around Ranger Brigade headquarters the day before, or knew of any other women being attacked or harassed in the park. None of them recognized the biker Carmen described, either.

They met Randall Knightbridge and Lotte hiking out of the canyon when they returned to headquarters. "We tracked her as far as the river," Knightbridge said. He took a water bottle from his pack and filled a bowl for Lotte, then drank himself. "We spent a lot of time looking around there, but Lotte couldn't pick up anything."

"You're sure the trail headed to the river, not from the river up to the road?" Reynolds asked.

"I'm sure."

"Then I'm even more sure Trask is involved in this," Reynolds said.

"We know he's hiding out somewhere here in the park," Knightbridge said. "This gives us somewhere to focus our search."

"What could he want with Faith?" Carmen asked. There were so many terrible answers to that question. She sent a silent message. *Hang on, Faith.* The Ranger Brigade may not have done its best to make her feel welcome before, but she was one of them all the same and they wouldn't stop until they found her. All she had to do was hang on.

FAITH LAY AGAINST the wall in the cave, listening to Dane Trask's steady breathing as he slept. At least, she thought he was sleeping. She could see nothing in the utter blackness of the cave, a disorienting feeling that had left her fighting panic after he had switched off the lantern. She had braced herself with her hands against the floor, as if at any moment she might plummet into a heretofore unseen pit. Closing her eyes had helped, and focusing on the sounds around her—her unsteady breathing and then Dane's more steady inhalations and exhalations. The cave smelled of dust and the remnants of their chicken dinner, of leather boots and smoky cotton.

Gradually, her racing heart slowed and she was able to open her eyes and relax her tensed muscles. But she couldn't sleep. Her ballistics vest dug into her and the floor itself was hard and cold. Not that she believed she could have fallen asleep with a man she didn't trust so close beside her, even though she was pretty sure he wasn't going to hurt her. She didn't agree with his method of getting her attention, but he'd exhibited none of the erratic behavior or desperate physical gestures Jerry Dallas had exhibited when he had held her captive. Dane had presented his case to her calmly and logically, and she'd believed him when he'd said he'd meant her no harm. But she didn't trust him. After seven weeks living on his own, running from real or imagined enemies, she couldn't judge how stable he really was.

Though he had left her unrestrained, he had positioned himself between her and the cave entrance. But she had long since given up the idea of trying to get away from him in the darkness. Even slung over his shoulder and fighting panic, she had noted the steep drop-off on the climb to this cave. She had no idea where she was and trying to find her way in the dark would be foolish.

Faith closed her eyes again, and may have dozed from time to time, but spent most of the silent hours mentally replaying as much of their conversation as she could remember. His story had been as wild as any conspiracy theory she had read, yet parts of it had the ring of truth. She was aware of an uptick in drug trafficking in the area in the past two years. She had seen the results multiple times during her tenure with the sheriff's department. But authorities had always placed the blame on Mexican cartels flooding the American market with cheap product. She had never considered that a reputable company like TDC might be profiting from the misery heroin caused.

She shifted again on the hard floor. The blanket he'd given her was thin and, while warm, did little to cushion her. "You should take off that ballistics vest." His voice broke the silence, deep and gentle. "It can't be comfortable."

She didn't answer.

"I promise to close my eyes," he continued. "I may not look it, but I can be a gentleman."

The teasing note in his words made her smile. "I'll leave it on," she said. "It must be almost morning."

"Almost," he said. "Though it takes a while for the sun to reach down here, and of course, it's always dark in the cave."

"Are we at the bottom of the canyon?" She remembered them traveling down then up.

"Nearly."

"How did you find this place?"

He paused, then, instead of answering the question, asked, "What do you do when the stress of your job—or life in general—gets to you?"

"I watch British TV," she said. "And read British novels." Why had she told him that? None of the people she worked with—even those she counted as friends—knew about her fascination with Jane Austen, Thomas Hardy, *Rumpole of the Bailey*, *Poldark* and others.

"I go backpacking," he said. "I like being away from other people and traffic and the news. Since I got out of the army and moved here, I've come to Black Canyon of the Gunnison. I've probably spent three hundred nights or more camping all over the backcountry. I found this place a year or so ago. I even slept here a couple of times. Then, after I learned what I did about TDC, I stashed some supplies here, just in case I needed a place to run to."

"You were an Army Ranger," she said. "I remember reading that."

"Yes. The training the army gave me has come in handy, but I've always loved the outdoors, and I've never minded living alone. Sometimes I prefer it. If something goes wrong, I'm the only one to blame."

"It sounds lonely." It was one thing to be independent, but there were times when the desire for someone else to rely on, confide in and simply be with—was a physical ache. Surely, he felt that, too.

"I never thought to ask," he said. "Do you have a family? A husband? Children?"

"No."

"Parents? I'm sorry if I've worried them. I forget, not everyone is unattached, like me."

"My parents were killed in an automobile accident ten years ago," she said.

"You must have been very young."

"I was fourteen."

"I'm sorry. That's a tough age to be on your own."

"Yes." With no relatives to take her in, she had ended up in foster care. No one had wanted to take in a disgruntled teen who was so desperate for a place to belong. She'd found that belonging in law enforcement. Not that she had made any close friends, but her fellow officers were her family, and she had been confident they would always be there for her.

"The Ranger Brigade will be looking for me when they discover I'm missing," she said.

"I meant what I said last night—when it gets light enough to hike the trail safely, I'll take you part of the way. You can go back and tell them what I told you."

"You should come with me," she said.

"It isn't safe."

"We can keep you safe."

"I don't think you can."

She sat upright and leaned back against the wall. "I think you underestimate us," she said.

"And you underestimate the people who are after me." He shifted position, too, fabric dragging against stone as he rearranged the sleeping bag. "Yesterday morning, I was attacked by a man who tried to kill me. He wasn't one of those amateurs out for the reward TDC is offering. He was a professional. I managed to fight him off."

"Is that the reason for your busted lip and bruises?" she asked.

"Yes. If a man like that can find me out here, I don't stand a chance back in civilization, where I'm easy to locate. I can't be sure who is and isn't on TDC's payroll."

"The Rangers aren't," she said.

"I want to believe you, but I'm not going back until I'm certain the people responsible have been arrested and put where they can't do me any harm— or my daughter. I can fend for myself, but I can't put her in danger."

"Do you know she's seeing a Ranger officer?" she asked. "Mark Hudson is a good man and he'll keep her safe."

"I saw them together at the press conference. I'm glad she has someone else to look after her, but I'm not going to take any chances."

Would she feel the same in his shoes?

"I owe you an apology," he said.

For tying her up and dragging her down here? Or for something else? "I'm listening."

"I shouldn't have forced you to come with me. Now that I've had time to think about it, and especially now that I've remembered who you are—it was really wrong of me. I'm sorry for putting you through this. I hope you won't hold it against me."

"What do you mean you remembered who I am?"

"Lying here tonight, I remembered the news reports last year about a female cop who was held hostage and severely beaten. I realized that was you, and it made me sick to think I made you relive that experience in any way."

His concern touched her. Emotion constricted her throat and it was a moment before she could speak.

"I'm okay," she said. "This isn't anything like that experience."

"You saved that little boy's life," he said. "You really are a hero."

"I risked my life, and the lives of others foolishly," Faith said. "I thought because I knew the boy's father—he was a childhood friend—that I could make a difference when other, more experienced, officers, couldn't. I heard later that my going in there probably made the situation worse. It angered him to the point where he might have killed me and the child."

"But he didn't," Dane said. "I think the end results are more important than all the things that could have gone wrong."

No one had ever said that to her, and she had never allowed herself to think it. "Thank you," she said. "I'm not sure anyone else saw it that way."

"I'll bet the boy's mother did. And the boy himself, when he's old enough to consider it."

"Maybe you're right. I hope so." Talking with him like this, so close she could hear every movement but unable to see him at all, had a curious intimacy. His deep voice vibrated through her, gentle and soothing.

Light flashed and she realized he was looking at his watch. "It's after six," he said. "Let's have breakfast, then I'll show you the way out of here."

He lit the lantern then dug out a one-burner backpacking stove and set water to heat. He handed her a headlamp. "Put this on and you can walk along the ridge a little ways to a stand of brush where you can relieve yourself. Just be careful on the loose rock."

She stood, muscles protesting after so long on the hard ground. The blackness began to give way to gray as she moved toward the entrance to the cave. Outside, she paused to survey her surroundings. Brush obscured the mouth of the cave, and the ground slanted backward, so that anyone standing below would have been unable to see inside. She eased past the brush, along a foot-wide ledge littered with loose gravel, until she found a thick stand of oak brush. She jumped as a striped ground squirrel darted across her path, and realized how on edge she still was. How had Dane lived like this for seven weeks, always alert for people who wanted to kill him?

The river, still in darkness, gurgled below her, and a robin trilled its morning song from somewhere in the rocks above. The air smelled of piñon and juniper, bracing and fresh. Faith felt stronger now, more sure of what she had to do next.

The Ranger Brigade would be looking for her soon. In a couple of hours, when officers started reporting for work, they would see her car in the lot, her belongings where she had dropped them. So far, they hadn't been able to find Dane by himself, but two people together were harder to hide. Not that she wanted to hide with him. But she wanted time to collect the evidence she needed to bring this case to an end.

Dane was crouched beside the stove, pouring water over coffee grounds, when she returned. "It's a beautiful morning," she said.

He looked up at her, the bruises on his face purpling, yet they did little to detract from his good looks. He wouldn't have been out of place in the pages of a men's magazine, modeling hiking gear or adventure expeditions. "You came back," he said. "I wasn't sure you would."

"I want you to take me to where you've hidden the proof of what you've learned about TDC," she said. "I need those videos and photos to make my case to the Rangers."

"I'm not sure that's safe," he said. "I can tell you where I've hidden them, but you'd probably have to get a warrant to retrieve them."

"I'm not going to get a warrant on my secondhand account of what you've told me." She crouched until she was looking him in the eyes. "All the talking in the world does no good without proof," she said. "I need that evidence."

He nodded. "All right," he said. "But it's going to be dangerous."

"I'm not afraid of danger," she said. He needed someone on his side. By default—and by choice— that person was going to be her.

Chapter Eight

"We're looking for his woman, possibly in the company of this man." Carmen passed the flyer with photographs of Faith and Dane to the white-haired couple camped in a Sprinter van in the BLM camping area.

The wife peered over her husband's shoulder at the photos. "That's a nice-looking couple," she said.

"What did they do?" the man asked. "Why are you looking for them?"

"The woman is a law enforcement officer," Carmen said. "She may have been abducted by the man." Carmen turned over the flyer in her hand, which included an artist's rendering of a long-haired, bearded man with aviator glasses and a bandana around his head—a likeness of the man Carmen had seen staring at Faith at the press conference outside Ranger headquarters. "We'd also like to know if you see this man," she said. "The woman may be with him or he might be alone."

"Oh, that's terrible," the woman said. "Do you think it's dangerous for us to stay here? Should we move to another area?"

"I don't think you're in any danger, ma'am," Carmen said. "Call the number on the bottom of that flyer if you see anything."

She left the couple and headed back to the cruiser, where she met up with Hud. "Any luck?" she asked, nodding to the stack of flyers in his hand.

He shook his head. "We're not going to find them this way," he said.

"This was the last place Dane Trask may have been," Carmen said. "It's possible he's moved out of the park and is hiding somewhere near here."

"It's possible he's fled to Mexico," Hud said. "Not likely, but that's the whole problem with this case. He's been hanging around the park for seven weeks and we still have no idea where he's hiding out or how he's surviving."

"Or why he took Faith," Carmen said.

"Or even if he took her," Hud said. "Maybe that biker you saw took her. Or someone else."

"I don't think it's a good sign that we haven't had any kind of ransom note," Carmen said.

Hud nodded. "If whoever took her killed her outright, they wouldn't bother with that."

"We haven't found her body or any sign of murder," Carmen noted. She tried to tell herself that was a good sign, but with so many acres of wilderness where Faith's captor could have taken her, the idea wasn't much comfort.

"Come on," Hud said. "There's one more camper up here. He just pulled in."

Together, they walked to the van parked beside a

rock outcropping. A slender man with close-cropped gray hair looked up from laying a campfire. "Hello, Officers," he said.

"We're looking for some people who may have been in this area." Hud handed him the flyer. "The woman is a Ranger Brigade officer who was abducted yesterday. She may be with the man in the photo next to hers there, or with someone who resembles the sketch on the back."

The man stood and took his time studying both sides of the poster. He shook his head. "Sorry, I haven't seen them. But there was a guy here last night who looked pretty rough. Made me a little uneasy, you know?"

"Rough how?" Carmen asked.

"Like he'd been in a fight. He was really banged up. And he was wearing a big pistol, right out in the open. I guess that's not illegal here, but it didn't make me want to get too close to him. He just looked mean, you know?"

The hair on the back of Carmen's neck rose. Some people had good instincts about strangers. Maybe this man was one of them. "Could you describe the man for me, Mr....?" she asked.

"Jackson. Del Jackson." He tilted his head to one side and closed his eyes. "He was a big guy—maybe six-four, over two hundred pounds. But I got the impression it was mostly muscle, not fat. He was in his midthirties, I'd say. A white guy, with either really short hair or bald. He wore a dirty ball cap and jeans and a chambray shirt. But like I said, he looked like he'd been in a fight—dirty clothes, swollen jaw, scraped knuckles. He was camped back there in an old pickup—that kind of mint green color you used to see in old cars, with a lot of primer." He gestured toward the far end of the road. "I like to take a walk before I turn in for the night and I passed him and said hello and he just glared at me. Gave me the creeps."

"Can you give us your contact information, in case we need to get in touch with you again?" Carmen asked.

Jackson gave them his address and cell phone number, and Carmen also noted the plate number on his van before she and Hud retraced their steps through the camp to the last turnout on the rutted road. Tire tracks through the grass showed where someone had parked in the space between two clusters of piñons. Rocks had been piled to make a fire pit, which was littered with half-burned trash: light beer cans, the wrapper from a convenience store burrito and a package that had contained chocolate-covered donuts. Hud knelt beside the fire ring and poked at the ashes. "There's still some warmth in here," he said. "He didn't leave that long ago."

Carmen studied the ground around the area. The red clay had been stomped smooth by years of campers, leaving no shoe impressions. She paused beside where the vehicle had likely been parked and stared at a trio of brown stains on the ground, each about the size of a quarter. "Come look at this," she said.

Hud joined her. "That looks like blood. We'd better get a crime scene team out here."

"Jackson said the camper looked like he'd been in a fight," Carmen said. "Maybe the blood is his."

"Maybe," Hud said. "But we'd better make sure."

Carmen had learned never to jump to conclusions when conducting an investigation. Let the evidence lead to the right solution. But that dispassionate focus on fact was harder to maintain when the case was personal. If that was the camper's blood on the ground, had Faith been the one to wound him?

And if it wasn't the man's blood, was it Faith's? Had they been this close to finding her and missed their chance?

"WE'RE GOING TO need a car."

Faith looked up from the leftover chicken in a tortilla wrap Dane had presented to her for breakfast. "Excuse me?"

"If we're going to get the photos and video for you to show to the Rangers, we're going to need a car," Dane said.

"Where are they?"

"At the Mary Lee Mine."

"You left them there?" She stared. "Where the people involved in the drug smuggling were supposedly spending a lot of time? Why?"

"Because they would never think to look for the evidence I had against them there." He scooted closer. "Look, if they were searching for the evidence, they'd look at my workplace, my house and on my person. Maybe with people who knew me, or at a safe-deposit box I had."

She'd almost forgotten about that safe-deposit box—yet another red herring the Rangers had had to chase down. "You sent your girlfriend a key to that box," she said. "She thought it was because you had left something important in there."

"Former girlfriend. And I did that to throw off TDC." He stuffed the last of his own chicken wrap into his mouth and chewed while she waited for the rest of his explanation. She sipped coffee, trying not to make a face at the bitter taste.

"Let me guess," he said. "You're more of a latte gal."

"I prefer cream and sugar," she said. It would take a ton of both to make this particular brew palatable.

"I guess I got used to strong and black in the army," he said.

"Mmm. At least this should keep me awake. Now, about that safe-deposit box?"

"Right. I made the mistake of hinting to Ruffino that I had information about his activities tucked away in a safe place, in case anything happened to me. I thought the threat might induce him to back off. Instead, he went after me and the information, so I decided to divert his attention to the safe-deposit box. And he fell for it. If you remember, one of Ruffino's henchmen got to the box and opened it before Eve could get there."

"What was in the box?"

"A bunch of garbled reports about the school building site. I hoped that if Eve retrieved them from the box first, she would turn them over to authorities and someone there would take a closer look. That's what all of this has been about—trying to get law enforcement to figure out all this on their own. I was trying to provide hints."

She gave up on the rest of breakfast and pushed it aside. "A direct statement would have been much more helpful," she said.

"Maybe. But I think my way was safer."

He would. She was beginning to see that once Dane Trask fixed on an idea, he was reluctant to shift his focus. That kind of determination may have served him well in the military, and even in his career, but it had complicated the Ranger Brigade's investigation in all kinds of ways.

"So you left the pictures and video at the mine?" she prompted.

"There's a flash drive with the information hidden in the mine tunnel. Near where they were storing the heroin. But it's miles from here. We need a car."

"No," she said. "First, we need a plan."

"I have a plan," he said. "We go to the mine, retrieve the flash drive, I give it to you and you give it to the Rangers. I continue to lay low until the people responsible for all this are arrested."

"You make it sound so simple," she said. "Do you have paper and something to write with?"

"Why?"

"If you want my help, you're going to have to humor me," she said. "I think better on paper."

He shoved to his feet, went and dug around in a large backpack and returned with a spiral notebook and a pencil. "Don't make this more complicated than it needs to be," he said.

"Says the man who, instead of coming right out and reporting illegal activities when he had the chance, wrecked his truck, abandoned his life and instigated a seven-week manhunt."

Dane glared at her and she glared right back. "Don't talk to me about complicated," she said. "We're going to do this right, and in a way that keeps both of us as safe as possible."

She opened the notebook to a fresh sheet of paper. "We need to establish our objective, then list the steps we have to take to get there," she said. "Then we can think about possible obstacles and how to overcome them. We may have to make adjustments in the field, but this will give us a good start." She wrote "Objective," "Steps" and "Obstacles" on the paper. "I'm surprised you didn't think of this before. You're an engineer."

"I had a plan," he said again.

"Your plan was suffering from tunnel vision." And maybe a lack of awareness of how other people— namely TDC—were likely to act.

"Do they teach this in the law enforcement academy?" he asked.

"No. Foster care."

He frowned. "You were in foster care?"

"After my parents died. There was a class on 'life skills' that was supposed to help us once we aged out of the system at eighteen and were on our own. For most kids, it was like being thrown into the deep end of the pool without knowing how to swim. They either figured out really quick how to keep their head above water or they didn't. Someone in the local organization decided to give us classes in things like budgeting, how to handle money, things like that. One day they had a woman come in and talk about goal setting and planning. It struck a chord with me."

"What was your plan?" he asked.

"My plan for what?"

"For your life?"

Faith pretended to focus on the page, drawing neat lines. "I knew I needed an education. I had a little money my parents had left me and I started looking for scholarships. After I graduated, I went into the police academy then got a job with the Montrose County Sheriff's Office. It worked out."

"That's your career plan. What about the rest of it?" He was closer now, their thighs almost touching as they bent over the notebook. "Life isn't all about work."

"Maybe I'm a person who prefers to focus on one thing at a time." She traced her pencil over and over the words she had written.

"You're not the kind of woman who has to be alone unless you want to be," he said. "I'm not saying that's not a good option for some people, but what you said earlier, about the way I've been living sounding lonely, made me think you spoke from experience."

"Are you saying it's my fault if I'm not in a relationship?" She told herself she should look at him, to read the emotion behind his words, but the minute she raised her eyes to meet his, she was sure she had made a mistake. The wanting in his expression left her stripped bare. It wasn't raw lust—though desire was definitely part of it—but rather, a sense of being on the outside, wanting badly to be let in. An emotion that was as familiar to her as breathing.

"I'm not going to pretend I know what's going on in your head," he said. "That's a different kind of violation none of us needs. But when I look at you, I see a smart, attractive, strong woman. The kind of person who would be a real partner in a relationship. Whenever I go through stretches where I'm alone— like now—it's always because I'm protecting myself from hurt or the effort it takes to be with someone, or frustration at the way things haven't worked out before." He shrugged. "You're not me, but I feel we might have a few things in common."

Was he coming on to her? Personal confession as flirting? She looked away. No, this was something else. As if…as if he truly cared and wanted to help her. That was ridiculous, considering he'd known her less than twenty-four hours, and for much of that they had been adversaries.

Except, she felt that kind of a connection to him, too. Yes, he was stubborn and had caused her and her fellow officers no end of trouble with his wrong-headed approach to the illegal activities he had— allegedly—uncovered. But she believed he had been trying to do the right thing. And she knew all about protecting her emotions and avoiding complications in her life. It was no secret foster kids had trust issues. It sounded like Dane did, too.

"Maybe we have some things in common," she said. "That should help us work well together. So let's get started on our plan." And stop talking about personal issues. She wanted to focus on facts and strategies, and not think about the crazy emotions he was making her feel.

Chapter Nine

Charles Terrell, founding partner of Terrell, Davis, and Compton, looked like money, from his exquisitely tailored gray suit to his perfectly styled hair, touched with just the right amount of silver, and his neatly trimmed goatee. A Rolex glinted on his wrist, and a ring with a large diamond adorned one finger. He carried himself with the air of someone used to being listened to. He was respectful and polite, but Carmen couldn't help believing he thought he was doing them all a favor by gracing them with his presence.

"I'm hoping you can update me on the search for Dane Trask," he said, having stopped by Ranger Brigade headquarters that afternoon. "I heard about the female officer who is missing."

"Do you have some information for us about Officer Martin's disappearance?" Carmen asked. Since Faith's disappearance, the members of the Brigade had been taking turns fielding queries from the press and public. Today was her lucky day.

"You should focus your investigation on Dane

Trask," Terrell said. "This is exactly the sort of thing he would do."

Carmen frowned. "We haven't found anything in Trask's history that shows violence toward women," she said.

"She's not a woman to him," Terrell said. "She's a law enforcement officer. He'll do anything to stop you from discovering the extent of his illegal activities."

This was a familiar narrative, started by the late TDC vice president, Mitch Ruffino. Before his death and the revelation of the scams he had been involved in, he had tried to blame Dane Trask for everything from littering to murder. "What illegal activities, in particular, are you referring to?" Carmen asked.

"Were you aware that the Montrose County Sheriff's Office seized a truckload of high-grade heroin from a storage facility west of town yesterday?"

She managed to hide her surprise. "No. How do you know about it?"

"The truck was operated by a TDC contractor. Naturally, the sheriff's department questioned us about it. TDC would never be involved in anything like that." He shoved his hands in the front pockets of his suit trousers. "On further investigation, I discovered that Dane Trask had communicated with that same company. When he traveled to Mexico earlier this year to conduct testing at one of our construction sites down there, he apparently took time off the job to visit the trucking company headquarters. I believe this shows he is connected to the drug smuggling. It explains his sudden disappearance, his attempt to fake his own death—and his recent murder of Larry Keplar and the kidnapping of your officer." Terrell looked smug, as if he had just solved the whole case and she should be thanking him.

"We don't have any proof linking Trask to any of those crimes," Carmen said.

"Circumstantial proof is still proof," he said. "I'll be happy to share TDC's records with you, showing Trask's trips to Mexico—there were several. The trucking company owner will verify that Trask visited their Mexico facility. And I understand Trask's fingerprints were found on Larry's car."

The information about Trask's fingerprints had not been released to the public, and had not been reported by any media that Carmen was aware of. "How did you hear about that?" she asked.

"I can't remember. Someone brought it to my attention. I came here today to find out what you're doing about Trask. The man is causing more and more harm, the longer he remains on the loose."

"We are continuing our investigation," Carmen said.

"Have you issued a warrant for his arrest?"

Carmen assumed a stern expression. Charles Terrell might have a fortune backing him up, but she had a badge. "I don't think that's any concern of yours," she said. "We are pursuing all leads and we are looking at all the evidence. As for the smuggling—you'll have to talk to the sheriff's department about their case."

"I will. And I'll be talking to your supervisor, Officer Redhorse. I don't appreciate your obstructionist attitude." He turned and left, the windows rattling as he shut the door behind him.

Hud joined Carmen in front of her desk. "'Obstructionist attitude,'" he said. "I like that. It might make a good T-shirt."

"I don't like people who think they can throw their weight around just because they have money," she said. "And I'm really annoyed that someone is leaking information about our investigations to that man."

"I saw a little item online about the tractor-trailer full of heroin the sheriff's department confiscated," Hud told her. "It didn't mention it was from a TDC contractor."

"Terrell probably made sure of that," she said.

"You didn't tell him we'd pretty much ruled out Trask for Larry Keplar's murder," he said.

"He's still on the suspect list, just not very high up on it," Carmen said. "My money is on that rough-looking camper Mr. Jackson told us about."

"I just talked to Reynolds. He's over at Blue Mesa Reservoir today, dealing with a fight between two fishermen that ended up with one slicing up the other with a fillet knife."

She winced. "Ugly."

"Yeah, well I was telling him about our mysterious camper and he said he and Faith and Beck talked to a man who matched that description, right down to the truck he was driving. He gave his name as Mike Stacy and his truck was registered to Wendell Stacy of Ohio. The phone number he gave was bogus and no one has been able to reach either Mike or Wendell. The commander just put out an APB for him. If we're lucky, someone will spot him on the highway and bring him in."

"He's the person I most want to talk to about Faith's disappearance, too," Carmen said.

"I heard the blood we found isn't Faith's," Hud said.

"No, but Lotte and Knightbridge followed a trail of more blood back into the woods behind the camp, to where it looked like there may have been a fight," she said. "They're running tests of other bloodstains found there, hoping they can figure out who the other person involved was."

"It wasn't Keplar," Hud said. "The ME said there wasn't a scratch on him."

"No, but it could have been Faith's."

Hud looked skeptical. "Faith is what—five foot two? Granted, she has some training, but by all reports, Stacy was armed, and probably weighed twice what she does and was more than a foot taller."

"I'm not assuming anything at this point," Carmen said.

"That's interesting about the heroin shipment," Hud said. "Though it's not the first time they've been seized around here. I know from my time with the DEA that there's been an uptick in heroin shipments through here in the past two years. And it's interesting how often it's come up in relation to this case—the private investigator who was spying on Audra Trask had heroin in his car. After Dane Trask's house was broken into, they found heroin, which hadn't been there before when they'd searched the house. And then Keplar died of an overdose."

"If Trask was involved in distributing heroin, where did he hide the money?" Carmen asked. "We've been through all his financials. There's nothing there. His only income is his salary from TDC. He lived simply. His truck was the most expensive thing he'd ever purchased, as far as we could tell. The FBI's forensic accountants went through everything and nothing suspicious popped."

"The DEA hasn't been able to establish any local link to the shipments they've seized," Hud said. "They've busted some small-time dealers, but everything else leads back to Mexico."

"It's curious that this truck was a TDC contractor," she said.

"Not really. Those contract haulers work for a lot of people. This one probably wasn't exclusive to TDC. Maybe he hauled equipment or something to a TDC job in Mexico and one of the cartels offered him big bucks to carry heroin back to the States. Maybe they thought because he worked for a company like TDC, an international concern with a good reputation, he'd be less likely to be stopped."

"Maybe," she said. "But from the start of this case, I've wondered why TDC has been so intent on making Trask out to be a villain."

"Because he tried to expose their dirty dealings at the Mary Lee Mine."

"Which they insist was all Ruffino's doing, not company sanctioned."

"It's always convenient to place the blame on a dead guy," Hud quipped.

"It doesn't seem as if their reputation has suffered much," Carmen said.

"They've been spreading the money around," Hud said. "I saw in the local paper that they just made a big donation to the new cancer wing at the hospital."

And everybody was singing TDC's praises. Maybe her job made her cynical, but Carmen doubted the company's motivations. "When I was a kid and I tattled on my brothers, my mom would say I only made her want to look closer at what I had been up to," she said.

"Are you saying you think TDC is trying to focus our attention on Dane Trask so we don't look too closely at them?" Hud asked.

"I think it wouldn't hurt to keep an eye on them."

"How are we going to do that?" he asked. "We're supposed to be searching for Faith, and Mike Stacy, and solving the murder of Larry Keplar. And finding Dane Trask—along with dealing with the occasional knife fight or smuggling operation or whatever else comes our way."

"I didn't say we had to focus on TDC," she said. "I'm only going to keep my eyes open for connections between them and our other cases."

"I'll add them to my list," Hud said. "Though big companies like that have enough layers, and enough lawyers, to put a lot of distance between us and them."

"I'm just going to be watching them," she said. Her father and brothers all liked to hunt deer and elk. *A good hunter is a good observer*, her father said. She would be a good observer, too, of a different kind of prey.

"It took them long enough to leave," Dane whispered in Faith's ear, one warm hand on her shoulder. They had been crouched in a stand of scratchy oak brush for the better part of two hours, waiting for the last car to leave the Ranger Brigade headquarters parking lot.

"They're probably working late looking for me," she said. "Or you."

"They can't know you're with me," he said. "Why would they?"

"Because they're smart," she said.

"And because I'm suspect number one in any crime that happens around here." His hand slid from her shoulder. "I read the papers. I know what people say about me. Most of it isn't true."

"If you don't like the rumors, step forward and end the speculation," she said.

He scowled and said nothing. She turned to study the parking lot again. In compliance with Dark Skies regulations in the county and around the national park, no security lighting illuminated the parking lot. The Ranger Brigade fleet vehicles—the ones officers didn't take home with them at night—were secured behind a tall fence and a locked gate.

The front visitor's lot, where most of the staff parked during the day, was empty, her Subaru gone, probably hauled off to the impound lot, where it would have been dusted for fingerprints and thoroughly inspected. But Dane had never touched the vehicle, so the Rangers wouldn't have found his fingerprints there.

"We need to get hold of one of those vehicles," Dane said.

"I don't know if stealing from a law enforcement agency is going to add to your cred." Faith had agreed to go along with this part of their plan because she saw no alternative, but she didn't like it.

"It's not stealing," he said. "You're a member of the Ranger Brigade. You're authorized to drive one of their vehicles."

"I need this thing called a key," she said.

"You know where the keys are kept, don't you?"

"Right. Inside that locked building." She had pointed all of this out to Dane when he had first proposed this method of obtaining transportation, but he had dismissed it all. Now that they were right up against these obstacles, he still refused to give in. The man was the very definition of stubbornness!

"I can see the back door from here," he said. "There's a keypad. I bet you know the code."

"We still have to get over the fence," she said.

"That's not going to be a problem." He slapped her on the back. "Come on. Follow me."

She was tempted to remain where she was and let him set out on his own. Once he was over that fence, she could even slip off into the darkness and run away. But the impulse was fleeting. She wanted to see this out. She wanted to get that proof and stop TDC from breaking the law with such impunity. If doing that required following the lead of this obstinate, reckless man, then so be it.

She sprinted after him across the deserted parking lot, to the fence. It was chain link, topped with two strands of barbed wire set at an outward-leaning angle. Dane didn't hesitate, but scrambled up the fence. At the top, he removed his light jacket, draped it over the barbed wire, and carefully levered himself over. He left the jacket in place and climbed down the other side. "Come on over," he said to her.

Faith didn't have any trouble scaling the fence, but climbing over, even with his jacket still protecting her from the barbed wire, was more difficult than he had made it look. "Don't overthink it," he called up to her. "Just focus on getting to me."

Slowly, awkwardly, she made it over, and paused at the top to catch her breath, and to retrieve his jacket. "Thanks," he said when she returned it to him at the bottom. "I didn't like to leave evidence behind."

She shook her head and looked toward the door and the shadows that now obscured the keypad. "There's a camera," Dane said.

She had wondered if he would notice, but of course he would. And she realized now that he had chosen to go over a section of fence that wasn't within the camera's range. "What do you suggest we do about it?" she asked.

"I could shoot it out."

"Noise carries a long way out here," she said.

"Campers in the National Park campground might hear."

He looked around then bent and picked up a fist-sized chunk of rock at the base of the fence. "Give me some room," he said.

It took three tries, but on the third, he threw a perfect strike and knocked the camera askew, so that instead of aiming down at the door and its vicinity, it pointed up toward the roof. Faith gaped at him. "Okay, I'm impressed," she said.

"I played baseball in college," he said. "Not good enough for Major League, but decent. Come on, let's get going."

They hurried to the door, where she punched in her pass code. The lock clicked and they were in. Faith resisted the urge to linger, to take in the familiar sights and sounds of her workplace, which presented such a sharp contrast to the cave in which she'd spent the past twenty-four hours. Instead, she forced herself to move quickly, toward the cubby where the keys to the fleet vehicles were kept.

"Any cameras in here?" Dane asked.

She shook her head and selected a key. She debated telling him she needed something from her desk, or the jacket she had left in her locker. Taking something like that would signal to her coworkers that she had been here. That she was safe. Then again, if anyone checked, they would see she had used her pass code.

"Let's get out of here." He touched her arm, urging her back to the door.

Reluctantly, she let him lead her away. Maybe it

was better if the Rangers didn't know she had been there. It would give her and Dane more time to gather the evidence they needed.

Outside, she led the way to the vehicle she had chosen, an older FJ Cruiser with more than a hundred and fifty thousand miles on it. It served as a backup vehicle when one of the newer cruisers was in the shop, its sides scratched and dented from hundreds of patrols through thick brush, its seats torn and patched with duct tape, a thick layer of dust coating the dash. "Did you purposely pick the worst vehicle on the lot?" he asked.

"It isn't used much, so no one will miss it right away," she said as she fit the key into the ignition. The motor ground then caught, and she let out a sigh of relief. "When we get to the gate, you get out and open it," she said.

She felt better once they were through the gate. She stopped at the edge of the lot so Dane could retrieve his pack, with extra food and water, from the clump of brush where they had been hiding. He loaded it into the back and they were off.

"Do you know how to get to the mine?" he asked.

"I have a general idea, but you can direct me," she said. Full darkness had descended. The thick, inky darkness was like a blackout curtain over the world that people only knew when they ventured into wilderness areas where the light from cities and houses had no chance to penetrate. The headlights of the FJ cut a slim path through the blackness, illuminating the road and a narrow strip of gravel shoulder on either side. Occasionally, eyes glittered in the blackness as they passed deer, and once a raccoon waddled across the roadside for a few yards before it disappeared into the underbrush.

Dane let out a sigh.

"Does it feel that good to be in a vehicle again?" she asked.

"No. It feels good to be out in the open, not having to hide, at least for a little while."

Faith heard no self-pity in his voice, but the reality of his words hit her hard. This man had been on the run for almost two months now, alone in the wilderness with hundreds, even thousands, of people hunting him, some of whom probably meant him harm. How had he managed to stay sane, much less survive? "You're safe now," she said.

"Because you're going to protect me?" She couldn't read his expression in the darkness, but she thought he sounded amused.

"Because we're going to prove you're innocent," she said. "You'll be able to stop running."

"We'll see," Dane said.

She didn't blame him for his doubt. She tightened her hands on the steering wheel. He didn't know her very well yet. He didn't realize he wasn't the only stubborn person in this vehicle. He wasn't the only one determined to triumph over bad odds. Hadn't she been doing that for years now?

Chapter Ten

The moon had risen by the time Dane spotted the turnoff for the mine. He leaned forward and pointed to their left. "Turn up here."

Faith signaled and made the turn. As they drove out of sight of the highway, Dane's shoulders relaxed. He had been waiting, ever since they'd left Ranger Brigade headquarters, for someone to spot them and try to flag them down, or even to pursue them. "I was holding my breath, afraid we'd pass another Ranger," Faith said, confirming she had shared his fears.

"But we didn't," he said. "We're okay."

"Right." She uncurled her fingers from around the steering wheel and flexed them, then switched the headlights to bright. They illuminated a stark landscape of rock and sagebrush, a primitive architecture of wild beauty. An almost full moon spotlighted towering rock monoliths that cast black shadows across graveled washes and stands of stunted piñons. "How much farther do we have to drive?" she asked.

"A couple of miles up this road then turn right. That road takes you up to the mine. It will take a while to get there—the road is too rough to go very fast. TDC made some improvements, but the roads wash every time it rains."

She nodded, and kept the FJ at just above a crawl, gravel pinging on the undercarriage. Dane rolled down the passenger-side window and breathed in the sage-scented air. After a moment, Faith did the same. "Have you been out this way before?" he asked.

"No." She glanced at him, moonlight draining all the color from her fair skin, her eyes hidden by shadow, like a Kabuki mask. "It's only in the last couple of days that I've been involved in any real way investigating cases," she said.

"Why is that?"

"I was hired to serve as a liaison with the sheriff's department, and as the Ranger Brigade's Public Information Officer. I've spent all my time issuing press releases and arranging press conferences, answering media queries and things like that."

"Do you enjoy the work?" he asked.

She shrugged, a gesture that said *I don't mind*, but the way her brow furrowed made him think the real answer was *I hate it*.

"What changed that you're investigating cases now?" he asked.

She sighed. "I went to the commander and essentially told him I was tired of sitting behind a desk and I wanted to be treated like a full member of the team."

"I guess he listened."

"I think I surprised him, but yes, he listened. So I

still have the PIO and liaison duties, but at least I get to play a more active role."

Dane leaned forward and pointed out the windshield. "Turn left just up here. After about a mile, you'll see a gate. We'll need to park before you reach the gate and we'll walk from there."

She turned where he indicated and the headlights illuminated a large sign that declared Private Property. No Trespassing. Authorized Personnel Only. Violators Will Be Prosecuted. Several bullet holes pierced the sign. Faith steered around the deepest ruts, then slowed as a ten-foot-wide iron gate came into view. Chain-link fencing topped with barbed wire stretched on either side of the gate. "TDC built all this?" she asked.

"At taxpayer expense," he said. "Park over there under those trees. That should be out of range of the cameras." He gestured toward the camera mounted to one side of the fence.

"I thought TDC had completed the mitigation at the mine," she said. "They shouldn't have any reason to be up here—or to be monitoring that camera."

"But does the government have the staff, or the inclination, to keep tabs on what's happening at a remote site on public land?" He unfastened his seat belt and opened the passenger-side door of the FJ. "TDC has a habit of paying people to look the other way when it suits their purposes."

"Are you saying you believe they're still using this location to store drugs?" She came around the FJ to join him. He checked the pistol in its holster at his side, then opened his pack and pulled out the weapon he had taken from her earlier. "I'm going to trust you not to use this on me," he said, trying for a joking tone but not quite succeeding.

She took the gun, checked that it was loaded and tucked it in the holster on her hip. "Are you expecting trouble?" she asked.

"Better to be prepared and disappointed than surprised. Come on." He gestured to their left then set off into the brush. The full moon bathed the landscape in a twilight glow, making additional light unnecessary, as long as they watched their step. He moved at an easy pace, keeping watch for signs that anyone else was up there, breathing in the clean, sage-scented air. As Faith moved up alongside him, he caught the scent of flowers—violets or roses, maybe. Sweet and feminine. Distracting, but in a good way.

"Where, exactly, are we going?" Faith asked, her voice low, just above a whisper.

"The fence at the back of the property isn't this impressive," he said. "Easier to get over."

"How many times have you come up here like this? I mean, at night, sneaking in?"

"A couple. For a while they had an armed guard."

"They don't anymore?"

"I don't think so," he said. "Maybe. I guess it depends if they're still using the place to store drugs."

"It would have been nice if you had mentioned this before." He couldn't see her glare but he could feel it.

"There are two of us, and I've never seen more than one of them," he said.

They reached the point where the chain link stopped, replaced by five strands of barbed wire. He stepped on the bottom wire and held up the next strand for her to scramble through. Then she did the same for him. Being so short, she had an easier time of it than he did, but he made it through. "Which way?" she asked when he stood beside her once more.

"This way." They traveled slightly downhill, through heavy woods, across a shallow creek, until they reached a large clearing. They stopped on the edge of a clearing shorn of trees and covered in fine gravel heaped into berms.

"What is all of this?" Faith asked. "It's so...stark."

"The berms are designed to catch any water that trickles through possibly contaminated rock above and filters out the contamination before allowing the water to travel along concrete-lined ditches to rejoin the creek below," he said. He pointed to a series of man-made hills along the perimeter of the open space. "More contaminated rock is buried in heavy clay, there, sealing it off."

"Why didn't TDC hide the radioactive material from the school building site in berms like that?" she asked. "Or does that not work for radioactivity?"

"I think that's how they planned to dispose of it," he said. "But I found out about it first, so they decided to just dump it at that illegal dump site and hope no one would trace it back to them."

She looked out across the expanse of gravel. "I don't see any sign of a guard."

"Neither do I. Let's go."

He skirted the clearing, keeping close to the trees, until he reached the timber-framed structure that marked the original mine entrance. The entrance, approximately six feet tall and four feet wide, was a black hole in the rock. Dane pulled a headlamp from his pocket and switched it on, then swore.

"That gate looks new," Faith said over his shoulder.

The gate, made of thick bars about four inches apart, completely blocked the opening to the mine. "This wasn't here last time I was up here," he said.

"They hadn't finished the project then, right?" She wrapped her hand around one of the bars and tugged. It didn't move. "Blocking the entrance was probably one of the requirements before the EPA would sign off on the project," she said. "The bars are to allow bats and anything else living in the tunnel to come and go."

But they wouldn't allow him to come and go. Even Faith, slender as she was, wasn't going to get through those narrow gaps. He turned and scanned the area around them. "What are you looking for?" she asked.

"Something to cut through those bars."

"Unless somebody left a cutting torch up here, I think you're out of luck," she said.

"There might be something in that shack." He started toward a wooden shed once used to store equipment during the restoration.

"Dane, wait," she called, hurrying after him. But he hadn't come this far to wait. TDC kept thwarting him and he had had enough of it. He wanted to get that proof and see them put out of business once and for all. He wanted to get back to his normal life. Until now, living in the wilderness hadn't bothered him much. At times, he thought he even preferred it. He liked being in nature and testing himself this way.

But spending even this little bit of time with Faith had reminded him of everything he was missing with his solitary existence. Soft beds and good food—soft women who smelled of flowers.

He reached the shed and grasped the door handle, expecting it to be locked. But it was just a standard door, and he was certain he could break it down if necessary. Instead of resisting when he tugged at it, the door swung open. He switched on the headlamp and scanned the small space, which contained a small desk, some tools and a long shelf with something covered by a tarp.

Except the tarp was a blanket. And the something was a large man, who made a sound like a growl, sat up and reached for a gun.

Chapter Eleven

Faith cried out as Dane, moving backward, slammed into her. A bullet clipped the doorframe of the shack, and a second sent up a shower of dirt near Dane's feet. "Run!" he shouted, and pushed her forward.

She ran, scrambling up the hill and into the cover of the woods, a man's bellows of rage echoing around them like the cries of some wild animal. Shots followed them as they continued to race through the trees. Before long, they'd reach the fence. She scanned the darkness, desperate not to hit the barbed wire at a full run, yet not daring to slow down until the last second. Whoever was following them continued to fire sporadically, but shooting a handgun while running uphill in the dark would challenge even the best shot. Still, a random ricochet or lucky aim might kill either one of them at any second.

Faith spotted a large outcropping of rock and ducked behind it. Gasping for breath, she drew her Glock and steadied herself against the rock. When the shooter ran past, pursuing Dane, she could get behind him, and maybe have a chance of picking him off.

But Dane, looking back, apparently misinterpreted her move and came stumbling back after her. "Come on," he said, grabbing her arm.

"I'm not—"

He didn't wait to hear what she had to say, merely picked her up, threw her over his shoulder and resumed running.

She wanted to scream at him to put her down. Maybe hit him in the head with the butt of her pistol to try to knock some sense into him. But with the shooter crashing through the woods behind them, she didn't dare do anything to slow him down. Instead, she made sure she still had a firm hold on the gun. "When we get to the fence, stop a minute and let me get off a shot," she said. "This guy isn't even trying to sneak up on us."

Dane's answer was a grunt, which she took as agreement. Sure enough, when they reached the fence, he paused long enough to set her on her feet. He doubled over, hands on his knees, breathing hard. "Do you see him?"

"Yes." The shooter was a dark, bulky shape, moving through the trees. His muzzle flashed and they both ducked. Then she returned fire—one, two, three shots. The shooter stumbled, though whether because she had hit him or because he was surprised, she couldn't tell.

"Come on." Dane grabbed her shoulder. "Let's go."

She dove through the fence and he followed, readying to pick her up again. "Don't be stupid," she said.

"I can run faster than you can." Then, to prove it, she took off.

She expected the man—it must have been the guard, asleep in the little hut—to follow them. Instead, he shouted curses, sounding winded, but didn't pursue. Dane took a different route back to the FJ, one that offered more cover and took them along the creek for what must have been a couple of miles. By the time they emerged on the road, the moon was half hidden by clouds, and she was glad of the brighter gravel strip to guide them.

Neither of them spoke until they were at the vehicle. She unlocked the doors, started the engine and headed out of there as fast as she dared, tires spinning on gravel at every curve. When they reached the road they had followed from the highway, Faith left the gravel to bump over the rough ground, and parked behind a large rock outcropping, where she hoped they would be out of sight. Then she turned to Dane. "First of all, if you ever manhandle me like that again, I promise I will clean your clock. Understood?"

"I thought you'd stopped because you couldn't go any farther," he said. "I came back to save you."

"I don't need saving. I'm a trained law enforcement officer and I had a plan. I stopped behind that rock to let him run past me, then I was going to pick him off when he went by. Until you went all caveman and threw me over your shoulder—slowing us both down, I might add—I don't think he even knew I was there. You took away the biggest advantage we had."

He was silent, which only made her angrier. Maybe

she should have beaned him with her gun when she'd had the chance. "I'm sorry," he said. He wiped his hand over his face. "I guess I'm so used to being on my own, making my own decisions on the fly, that I'm not used to working with someone else."

"I want to help you," she said. "But if we're going to work together, you're going to have to trust me. And sometimes, you're going to have to let me take the lead."

Dane was silent so long she was sure she had offended him. Maybe the super-macho Army Ranger couldn't bear the idea of taking orders from a woman. Too bad for him, then. She could drive straight back to headquarters, put him in restraints and call for backup. No more wasting time with his ill-conceived plans and poorly thought-out actions.

"I want your help," he said again. "And you're right—you're a trained professional. I'm sorry I didn't respect that. No more manhandling, I promise. And I'll listen to what you have to say. I'll even follow your lead—when I can."

She wasn't thrilled about that last qualifier, but coming from him, it was probably a big step forward. "All right," she said. "Just so we're clear."

"We're clear," he said. "So what do we do now?"

"We can go back to headquarters and in the morning you can tell the rest of the Ranger Brigade what you've told me."

"Are they going to believe me?" he asked. "I don't have any evidence but my own story. Everyone at TDC has spent the past two months doing everything they can to discredit me, and they've been building up their own image at the same time. I'm convinced they've paid off judges and politicians and even local law enforcement to look the other way."

"The Rangers will believe you because they haven't been paid off. And because I believe you." She couldn't be certain of the latter—she was the newest member of the team and none of the others knew her that well. They might very well think she had fallen under Dane Trask's spell. But they were also smart officers who were focused on justice. She believed they would listen to Dane and compare what he said with what they already knew about TDC.

Dane shook his head. "Even if they believe me, they won't be able to get a warrant to do a more thorough search for evidence. They can keep a closer eye on TDC, but they won't be able to prove any of what I've said. I'm positive that as soon as they feel any heat, TDC will either move their operations or cease activity for a while until they're no longer being watched so closely. What they won't do is forget about me, or let me go without making sure I—and probably Audra, too—pay for damaging their reputation."

Faith heard the fear behind his words, even if she couldn't see his expression in the darkness. And as much as she wanted to believe she and her fellow law enforcement officers could protect him, he had planted a seed of doubt. "You can't go back to hiding in a cave and trying to send vague hints to get law enforcement to look in the right direction," she said. "That didn't work."

"No." He turned his head and stared out the window at the moonlit landscape around them. "Maybe I should forget the whole thing. Just disappear altogether."

A fist squeezed her heart, though whether from the despair in his voice or the thought of never seeing him again, she couldn't say. "We can find a way to get the proof we need to punish the people responsible at TDC," she said.

"We could go back to the mine with a cutting torch," he said. "Though we'd have to disable the guard first."

Trespassing. Destruction of public property. Assault on a civilian. The list of charges came to mind automatically. "While I'm willing to skirt the law for the sake of justice, I'm not going to ignore the legalities," she said. "Not to mention, that automatically taints the evidence in the eyes of the court. We need to find a legal way to gather proof of TDC's involvement in heroin trafficking."

"I'm willing to listen to whatever you have to say," Dane said. "But can we do it back in the canyon? I'm exhausted and I imagine you are, too. Not to mention, I'm feeling too exposed out here in the open. It will be dawn soon, there will be more traffic on the roads and more chance of someone seeing us."

That would mean staying with him longer. Allowing her coworkers and family and friends to believe she was still missing and possibly in danger.

But she wasn't in danger. And she truly wanted to help this man. "All right." She started the engine of the FJ. "We'll go back to your cave, get some sleep and come up with a plan in the morning." What that would be, she hadn't the faintest idea, but with her logical mind and his sharp but impulsive one, they were bound to come up with something.

FAITH SLEPT, but Dane could not. He had insisted she take his sleeping bag. She lay in it now, a slight figure beneath the green-quilted cover, only the top of her head visible, dark hair a shadow spilling onto the rock floor. He sat against one wall, his headlamp providing a narrow spotlight on the area of the topo map he'd spread out before him. If Faith woke up, she would think he was plotting their next move—that he'd taken her advice to come up with a plan.

Except he had no idea what to do or where to go next. He'd been charging forward all these weeks, sure that he was going about revealing TDC's guilt in the only way it could be done. Faith had shattered that illusion, showing him just how narrow-minded and misguided he had been.

He cradled his head in his hand, the weight of his own failings bowing him down. He wasn't an idiot. Most of the time his doggedness and willingness to keep going despite the odds worked in his favor. When he had decided to set up a local organization to help veterans, a lot of people had said he didn't have the money, wouldn't get the support, wouldn't be able to connect with the people who needed his services the most.

Dane had proved them all wrong. He had kept

going, refusing to give up. And at his job with TDC, he'd developed a reputation as a man who got things done. He cut through—or went around—regulatory red tape. He worked into the night to meet impossible deadlines. Dane Trask wasn't someone who took forever to make a decision. He determined to do something and did it.

But now—when the outcome mattered so much—his charge-ahead philosophy had only made things worse. He'd given TDC time to cover its tracks. Each wrong step he'd made had led to another, until he was so far off track he wondered if he could ever get back.

His boneheaded idea to kidnap a Ranger Brigade officer was his latest poor decision. But he couldn't call it a mistake. He lifted his head to watch Faith sleeping. She pulled at something inside him, loosening a knot he hadn't even realized he was carrying around. One of the reasons he had selected her as the officer he would approach was that she was so small and slight he'd known she'd be no match for him physically.

But he'd judged her wrong. She, too, wasn't one to back down, and what she lacked in physical stature she made up for in courage and levelheadedness. She hadn't hesitated to point out everything he was doing wrong. Her words had stung, but looking past his wounded pride, he had seen she was right.

She stirred and her head emerged from the sleeping bag. She opened her eyes and looked at him. "What are you doing?" she asked.

He opened his mouth to tell her he was studying

the territory, planning a new approach, but honesty came out instead. "Mostly, I've been thinking about what an idiot I've been."

She shoved into a sitting position. Her face still wore the softness of sleep, and her hair was tousled, the way some women looked after sex. He turned his head away, desire a hard fist below the belt.

"Let me see that map," she said, and crawled the short distance across the cave to join him. She sat with her shoulder brushing his, the soft scent of her overwhelming him. She bent forward and studied the map. "What's this you have circled here?" She indicated a light brown rectangle at the far edge of the map, surrounded by the green of public lands.

"That's a private development where Charles Terrell has a second home," he said. "Or maybe it's a third or fourth home."

Her eyes met his, moss green in the light from his headlamp. "Have you been there?"

"No. I thought about going out there one day to have a look around, but never have."

"We should go there," she said.

"And do what?"

Faith gave half a shrug—only one shoulder moving. "We could confront him with what you know."

"I tried that with Mitch Ruffino, remember? And look how well that turned out."

She nodded, and continued to study the map, while he could focus on nothing but her—on the gentle curve of her ear and the pale softness of her neck that showed through the parted locks of her hair. She leaned forward and the side of her breast pressed against his arm, sending a jolt of awareness through him. Some time after they'd hid the truck and hiked back to the cave early this morning, she must have removed her ballistics vest.

She pressed against him even more. Was she doing it deliberately? He remained frozen, telling himself he should move away, but unable to do so. Then she turned her head and her eyes met his, and he felt the jolt of desire again, a wanting not unlike his own shining in her eyes.

He reached out to cup the side of her face, aware of the roughness of his fingers against her satiny cheek. Her lips parted—in surprise? Or invitation? Feeling reckless, he bent and kissed her.

The sound she made was halfway between a sigh and a supplication. He deepened the kiss, lips caressing, tongue teasing, until she opened for him, angling her head to bring them closer still. He moved his hand around to cradle the back of her head, fingers sliding in the silk of her hair. He wanted to wrap his arms around her—to wrap his whole body around her—but he restrained himself, the wanting and not yet having a pleasure of its own.

Faith made another noise—a low murmur in her throat—and pulled away. Reluctantly, Dane dropped his hand and let her go. He braced himself, prepared for her to give him another lecture about "man-handling" her. Maybe she'd even slap him. Maybe he'd even deserve it.

Relief filled him when she smiled. "Isn't that better than grabbing me and throwing me over your shoulder?"

He laughed, as much with relief as from the humor of the situation. He wondered if she'd be open to continuing where they had left off. Instead, she stood. "I'm starving. What do you have to eat?"

He was hungry, too, just not for food. But he followed her lead and stood, also. "I've got peanut butter and crackers. And some boiled eggs."

She made a face. "You've been living the life of luxury here, haven't you?"

He didn't answer, merely fetched the food from his stores.

While they ate, Faith studied the map again, tracing a route from their location to Terrell's property. "What are you thinking?" he asked.

"I think we should pay Terrell a visit tonight."

"He may not be there. I'm not sure how often he comes to the area."

"I bet he's there," she said. "He's been taking a personal interest in TDC's operations since Ruffino's death."

"What are we going to do when we get there? We won't be able to just walk in. The property is gated, and I'm sure there are guards. He may even have personal bodyguards. He'd be a fool not to."

Faith shook her head. "We're not going to confront him personally. We're just going to have a look around."

"What are we looking for?"

"Evidence of drug activity. I didn't see anything

to indicate TDC is still using the Mary Lee Mine to stash shipments of drugs. The road leading up to it isn't being regularly used, and though they have a guard there, he wasn't actively patrolling, or especially alert. That means they've moved storage to another location." She sat back, her gaze steady on him. "What better place to utilize than a big property that's already gated and guarded?"

Why hadn't he thought of that? He knew the answer—because he had been so focused on seeing things only one way. "You're brilliant," he said.

"Not brilliant," Faith said. "But I'm good at considering all possibilities." She folded the map then checked her watch. "We've got a couple of hours until it's dark enough to hike out of here to the truck. That will give us time to assemble everything we need."

He didn't ask what they would need—he was sure she would tell him. And for now, at least, he was content to follow her lead. Or at least, to protect her back. For a man who had prided himself for so long on going it alone, she was quickly becoming very important to him.

Chapter Twelve

Faith told herself not to overthink the kiss she had shared with Dane. It had been a nice little interlude—something they had both wanted at the time. It was a way of acknowledging the physical attraction between them, but it didn't mean they were going to take things any further. In a way, it had balanced the scales between them—a test that had proved he was willing, at least for now, to let her call the shots. If he had tried to pull her closer when she had ended the kiss, they would have had a different conversation afterward. Instead, he'd given in like a gentleman. For all the mistakes he had made to this point, he definitely had potential.

They loaded his backpack with extra food, water, the topo map, binoculars, a compass, a first-aid kit and extra ammunition. She put the ballistics vest back on and he loaned her a knit cap to pull down over her hair against the night chill. She had her weapon, phone, handcuffs and Maglite. Somewhere in their initial struggle, Dane had ditched her police radio, probably so she couldn't summon help. Now she hoped they wouldn't need any.

Guilt nudged at Faith whenever she thought of her fellow officers searching for her. She didn't want to worry them, but she needed a little more time with Dane to figure all this out. She didn't completely buy his argument that turning himself in would endanger his life and the life of his daughter, but she wasn't discounting his fear, either. If TDC had managed to conduct a multinational drug smuggling operation without anyone becoming suspicious, maybe they did have the resources to silence one man who many people already thought of as a dangerous nut.

"Are you ready?" Dane asked after he had shouldered the pack.

"I think so."

They had a three-mile hike ahead of them to reach the remote pull-off where they had stashed the Ranger Brigade FJ in a dense stand of trees. From there it was an approximate twenty-minute drive on mostly unpaved back roads to the highway, then a short trek to the gated entrance to the exclusive development Terrell had chosen for his local base.

The moon was up by the time they reached the FJ. "I don't think anyone has been here," Dane said, pulling branches away from the windshield.

Faith studied the ground around the truck, but everything looked undisturbed. "I'll show you the way to go," Dane said, sliding into the passenger seat as she started the engine.

Neither of them said much on the drive out of the

park, except when Dane indicated she should turn up ahead. Faith looked out at the moon-washed landscape and willed her body to relax. She recognized that the tension she felt now wasn't from fear, but from excitement. After so many weeks of spending too much time on mundane tasks behind a desk, she was finally going to be doing something risky and a little dangerous, but nevertheless important. The kind of work she had trained for.

A bird swooped low over the windshield and she let out a yelp. "Nighthawk," Dane said.

She nodded, her heart settling back into her chest where it belonged. "I knew they lived here, but I've never seen one before," she said.

"You have to be out at night. It's a different world out here then."

Though her job now involved protecting a vast wilderness, she had spent very little time exploring the sagebrush, rock and river that made this landscape different from any other she had lived in. Dane was at home in this world, and he was helping her to be at home here, as well.

They reached the highway and he instructed her to turn left. They didn't pass a single vehicle in the five miles to the turnoff for Sunset Estates. "Go past the main road in," Dane said. "There's a utility access we can take instead."

She slowed as they passed the entrance, drove around a curve and then spotted the entrance to a rough dirt track up ahead on the left. The track followed a fence line out of sight. "Where does this take us?" she asked, slowing to a stop but not making the turn.

"I've never driven it," he said. "But the map shows a cell tower and some water tanks at the top of the hill, so my bet is, it goes up there."

"Fair enough." She eased onto the track. It was rough going, the FJ bouncing in and out of deep ruts and over jutting rocks. As they neared the top of the hill, she switched off the headlights and cut her speed even more. They crested the top and came to a stop beneath a tall cell tower.

"We'll need to go in on foot," Dane said.

"Right." She turned the truck and backed in behind a pair of water tanks. Then, moving as silently as possible, they unloaded their gear from the vehicle and stood surveying their surroundings.

Even in the darkness, they could make out houses in the glow of security lights outside almost every residence. Faith counted five large homes and assorted outbuildings scattered across the hillside below. "Which one belongs to Charles Terrell?" she asked, keeping her voice low.

Dane took the binoculars from his pack and raised them to his eyes. Faith wondered how he could make out anything in this poor light, but after a moment, he lowered the glasses and pointed to the east. "The one at the very bottom of the hill, furthest to our left," he said.

"Are you sure?" she asked. "You said you had never been here before."

"I said I hadn't come out here to confront him. He

actually hosted a Christmas party for TDC employees and their families, shortly after the house was completed." He stowed the binoculars in his pack. "Come on. Let's see if we can get closer."

They avoided the street, instead sticking to a path that ran behind the homes, following stone walls and wrought-iron fences. "What is this path?" Faith asked.

"I think it's a bike or walking path," Dane said. "Probably one of the selling points for the neighborhood—green space and recreation opportunities."

"It's not very smart from a security standpoint," she said. "Not the way it provides access to every home."

"Lucky for us no one else pointed that out."

They moved silently past the still, dark homes. No dogs came out to sound an alarm. Faith supposed they were all inside with their owners, sleeping. The lots were large, several acres, she thought, some a little larger than others. Each was neatly fenced in a style that complemented the home—white limestone for one, wrought-iron pickets set between brick pillars at another.

"This is Terrell's," Dane said when they reached an arrangement of vertical logs, like the palisade on a Western fort.

They stopped to peer through gaps in the logs. The house was at least a hundred yards from this back corner, a flat-topped adobe structure that continued the Old West theme, rising two stories with parapets and a large second-story deck. Faith counted fourteen windows on this side of the house, as well as a hot tub and large patio paved with Mexican tiles. Everything glowed golden in the beam of a security light.

"I think what we're looking for might be in there." Dane pointed to a large Quonset hut in the far back corner of the compound. "That wasn't here at the party I attended."

"When was the party?" she asked, moving closer to him.

"Three years ago."

"You said the house was new. Maybe he added it as a workshop or hobby room."

"Maybe." He turned toward her. "He's married. His wife is an interior designer. She specializes in high-end homes. If she wanted to add a hobby room or a workshop or even a garage, I don't think she'd go for a Quonset hut."

Faith studied the half-circle structure of yellow-beige canvas that looked like a giant caterpillar stretched across the back lawn. "I see your point," she said. "So what is the Quonset doing here at all?"

"I think it's because it would be quick to erect, fairly cheap and is big enough to hide an eighteen-wheeler."

"Then we need to get in there and find out if your supposition is true," she said.

Dane started up the fence line again, but Faith reached out and grabbed the pack, pulling him back. "Let's scope out the situation better first," she said. "Plan our approach. Don't they do that stuff in the military?"

He nodded. "They also teach us to size up a situation quickly. There's a gate further down the fence, just before the Quonset hut. There's also a guesthouse at that end, which could house a guard or guards."

She nodded, impressed but determined not to show it. "All right then, what's your plan?"

"We make our way to the gate. One of us continues on up the fence line and around the side. I'm betting there's a gate somewhere on the street side where a big truck could pull in. Verify that and try to determine where the guards are located."

"That's a good start. Then what?"

"The person up front creates a diversion to distract the guards and the person back here gets through the gate and into the Quonset."

"What about the guard in the Quonset hut?"

His jaw didn't exactly drop, but he did look surprised. "You saw a guard in the Quonset?"

"No. But if I had a truckload of heroin in there, I'd have a guard on it. Wouldn't you?"

He folded his arms across his chest, muscles flexing. Distracted, she forced her gaze away. "I take it you have a better plan," he said.

"Not better. Just…more cautious."

"Let's hear it, then."

"If we split up, we each become more vulnerable," she said. "Better to stay together and work as a team. And if one person creates a distraction, that alerts the guards—including anyone who might be inside the Quonset—that an intruder is on the premises. We have a much better advantage if we can keep them from finding out about us as long as possible."

He frowned, so she added, "Your plan would work great if we had backup, but we're stuck out here by ourselves. We have to use stealth instead of force as much as possible."

"Right." The light caught the white of his teeth as he grinned. "Let's see if we can sneak in and get a better look."

"I like your idea of checking out up front first," she said.

He nodded then turned and began moving back along the fence. He stopped at the gate to check the latch. It was secured by a large padlock. Faith hefted the lock and shook her head, but didn't say anything, aware that anyone in the Quonset might hear them.

Dane led her to the corner of the fence, where they turned and made their way along the side. The logs forming the palisade-style barricade cast long shadows from the security light in the backyard. Faith was grateful for the shadows to help conceal them from view of the next-door neighbors, whose fence marched along parallel to this one, across a ten-foot open space she guessed was a utility easement.

The property was deeper than it was wide, and they walked a long way before they were within sight of the front of the fence and the street beyond. Dane halted and she moved in close behind him, peering around him. He looked down at her, one finger to his lips. She nodded and strained her ears, listening.

The scrape of something metal across wood—a chair pushed back in the guesthouse, which was just to their right. She pressed her cheek to the rough wood of the palisaded logs and peered into the back-yard. A faint glow showed beneath the drawn shades of the guesthouse, near the back. A night-light? No, something brighter. The light flickered and she realized someone inside was watching TV.

Dane tapped her shoulder and she pulled back from the fence. He pointed ahead and she nodded then followed him to the corner, where they both peeked around. The double gate easily spanned twelve feet. Enough room to pull in an eighteen-wheeler. But how would Terrell explain something like that to his neighbors? Maybe he didn't have to. Maybe the houses around him were also second homes, unoccupied for much of the year. If he was careful to time deliveries when his neighbors were away, no one would be the wiser. Terrell could also arrange for deliveries to arrive after dark, making them even less noticeable.

Dane moved away from her and darted to the gate. She bit back a caution and waited as he knelt in front of the gate and pressed his hand to the ground. He returned shortly, took her arm and led her back down the fence line. Only when they were some distance from the guesthouse did he lean over and speak. "There are fresh tracks in the soft dirt in front of the gate," he said. "Big tires, as if an eighteen-wheeler idled there while waiting for the gate to open."

Faith nodded. That would fit their hypothesis, but was that really what the evidence showed, or were they making assumptions to prove their theory? Confirmation bias was a problem in law enforcement as well as science. There was only one way to find out. "We need to get a look inside that Quonset hut," she said.

"I agree."

"But how are we going to do it?"

"The sides on those things are canvas," he said. "Thick canvas, but I've got a sharp knife. I think I can cut it and go in a way a guard inside won't be expecting."

It was a much riskier move than she would have liked, but she didn't see a better alternative. "We still have to get inside the fence," she said.

"I've got a plan for that, too," Dane said. He grinned again. "I think your penchant for planning is rubbing off on me."

"Let's hear your plan."

"I'd rather show you." He led her back down the fence and around the corner, toward the narrow, walk-in gate. But he didn't stop there. Instead, he hurried past the gate to the next adobe pillar. "These pickets are dug into the ground, then they're lashed together with wire," he said, pointing to the wires on a section of pickets. "But some of the wires are broken, and others can be cut. And before you ask—I've got a multitool with wire cutters on it. They won't handle heavy cable, but they'll be good enough for this gauge."

"The palisades are still sunk into the ground," she said.

"Not deep. And this one isn't deep at all." He tapped his toe against the base of the log on one side of the adobe pillar. "Plus, there's enough of a gap between the palisade and the pillar that I only need to remove one log to squeeze through."

She studied the gap and shook her head. "Criminals are sure they've thought of every angle," she said. "And then they find out they haven't."

He took off his pack and set it on the ground, then he opened it and took out the multitool. A few quick snips and the wire was loose. Then it was a matter of rocking the wood gently back and forth until he could yank it from the ground. "Can you whistle?" he asked her.

She started to fire back the old movie line about putting your lips together and blowing, but decided now wasn't the time. "Yes," she said.

"If anyone is coming or you hear anything, sound the alarm then take the pack and get out of here as fast as you can. Head back to the truck and I'll join you there when I can."

"Maybe you should wait out here and I should go in," she said. "I'm smaller than you, so I can get in places easier, and I'm wearing the body armor."

"And I'm the one who saw the drugs up at the Mary Lee Mine," he said. "I know what to look for."

She could have pointed out that as a law enforcement officer, she had seen plenty of drugs, but her heart wasn't in the argument. Dane had pursued this case for weeks, while she was a relative newcomer to the hunt. Why not let him keep going? "I'll wait and keep watch," she said. But if he thought she was going to run if trouble came around, he didn't know her very well at all.

DANE FORCED HIS body through the narrow gap between the remaining posts and the adobe pillar, scraping his back in the process. Once inside the perimeter, he paused, listening for shouts or footsteps, or the bark of a dog. Only his own pounding pulse echoed in his ears. On the other side of the line of vertical logs, Faith was a slight, dark shadow. A shadow his life might depend on. The idea didn't frighten him the way it once would have. After so much time—years, maybe even most of his life—of depending only on himself, it felt good to lean on someone else a little, even if he would never have admitted it aloud.

He moved away from the gap in the fence, toward the Quonset hut. This far corner of the yard was out of sight of the main house, which sat lower than the hut or the guesthouse on the sloping terrain. In addition to the Quonset hut and the guesthouse, this part of the property included an adobe hut he decided was meant for garden storage, judging by the collection of clay pots tumbled by its door, a couple of raised garden beds devoid of even weeds, and pieces of a cedar child's playscape stacked next to the shed.

The Quonset hut butted up against the back fence, with only a foot-wide gap between the canvas and the fence. Dane moved into this gap and discovered a wider space on the side, almost three feet between canvas and the palisades. He settled and dug out his knife. The glow from the security light didn't reach back here, so he had to feel his way in darkness. But he had only to put out his hand to touch the canvas of the Quonset, so he had no fear of getting lost. Instead, he plunged his knife into the fabric, sinking it to the hilt. Then he stopped again and waited.

No cries of alarm. No movement on the other side of the opaque canvas. No reaction from anyone.

Slowly, carefully, he sawed a foot down through the canvas, then across a foot, then up again. Forming an approximate twelve-inch by twelve-inch square that could be folded back to form a window into the Quonset. He tugged at the fabric, releasing the flap, which fell down. Then he peered inside. Blackness.

He waited for his eyes to adjust, but he still could see nothing inside the hut. He slipped on his headlamp and switched it on, taking care to shield the light with his cupped hands. Then he stuck his head into the opening he had cut in the canvas.

He looked out through a set of metal shelving. The shelves themselves appeared to line the sides of the Quonset, but they were all empty. The rest of the hut was not, however. It was filled almost completely with a large tractor-trailer rig, the silver sides of the trailer rising to almost brush the arched top of the Quonset.

So far, his suspicions about this Quonset hut—and Faith's suspicions about where Terrell had moved his operation—were holding up. But suspicion couldn't generate an arrest warrant. And it wasn't enough to stop Terrell and company. Dane needed proof, and he hadn't come this far to leave without it.

He switched off his headlamp and, keeping one hand on the canvas to guide him, moved down the side of the Quonset to the end against the palisade fence. He could barely squeeze into the space, but it was well hidden from anyone on the property, and it had another advantage. Like the other end of the structure, this one had a zippered canvas flap that could be opened and rolled up out of the way, to leave most of the end open. Dane knelt and found the zipper pull at the bottom corner and began to ease it up. Wary of making noise, he moved slowly, inch by agonizing inch. When he had opened the zipper to a height just over his head, he knelt again and found the tab for the zipper across the bottom. He slid this over a couple of feet and now had a flap he could easily fit through.

He stepped through the gap, and left it open, in case he needed to make a quick getaway. He put his hands out in front of him, and tried to remember what he had seen when he'd looked through the gap he had cut behind the shelving. He bumped into what had to be the back end of the trailer, and felt along until he came to a gap. Puzzled, he cupped his hands around the headlamp and switched it on once more.

He was standing against the bumper of the trailer. The back end had been rolled partway up to provide access to the trailer's interior. Dane scrambled up into this gap and crawled forward into the truck. The trailer was half full of blue plastic barrels. The nearest barrel was labeled with the chemical name for a popular fertilizer sprayed on the cornfields outside of town. Dane had seen the crop dusters dipping low over the fields as he'd driven past many times.

He examined the top of one of the barrels, then took out his knife and pried at the plastic cap over the only opening he found. He had to exert a lot of effort to work it out, but at last it was free and he removed the light from his head and directed the beam inside. No fertilizer, liquid or otherwise, but stacks of white and grayish bricks wrapped in thick plastic.

Heroin. Just like the stash Dane had seen in the Mary Lee Mine. He pulled out his phone and snapped off half a dozen pictures—of the contents of the barrel and the barrel itself. Then he replaced the lid and stepped back, and tried to estimate how many barrels of drugs were in this one trailer. They were stacked double, filling two-thirds of the trailer, held in place with heavy metal strapping, except for this one barrel that sat in a gap between the door of the truck and the rest. Maybe this barrel had been left out for the buyer to test the quality of the merchandise.

He snapped off a few more pictures then turned to go. He'd try to get photos of the outside of the trailer and of the license tag, if there was one. Then photos of the Quonset hut. The pictures, along with his testimony and Faith speaking on his behalf, ought to be enough to spur the Ranger Brigade into action.

He moved back to the opening and turned to lower himself to the floor. His feet had just touched the dirt when something sharp jabbed him, sending pain up his spine.

"Don't move," a deep voice said. "Or you're a dead man."

Chapter Thirteen

Dane was taking a long time. Faith forced herself to stand still by the opening in the fence, aware that movement was more likely to draw attention. But inside, she was pacing, and worrying about what reckless thing Dane might have done this time. The man had little regard for his safety, and a history of making rash decisions. He wasn't used to thinking about how the choices he made affected others. How his choices affected her.

She checked her watch, squinting to make out the numbers on the display. He'd been in there twenty minutes—more than enough time to take a look and get back out. Should she go in after him? She stepped forward, intending to squeeze through the gap in the fence, then froze as voices drifted to her, the words clear in the still night air. "This is going to be like last time," one man said. "A raccoon or something. I told TJ that perimeter alarm was set too sensitive."

"As long as it isn't a bear, I don't care," a second voice said. "But we have to check it out."

Faith swallowed a gasp then stared at the fence. Why hadn't they looked for an alarm?

But looking now, she saw no wires or sensors or electric eyes. They must be on the inside. And it didn't matter, anyway, because two men were headed this way. She sprinted out from the fence, to the cover of trees, and lay flat on her stomach in what might have been a drainage ditch. When a powerful flash-light's beam swept the area behind the fence, she squeezed her eyes shut, biting her lip as one of the men exclaimed over the gap beside the pillar. "Some-one cut the wire!" he said, his voice carrying in the clear night air. Would Dane, wherever he was, hear him and take cover?

The men's voices moved away and, after a long interval, Faith risked rising up and looking around. She saw no one. Of course they wouldn't be interested now in anything outside the fence. They were looking for someone who had broken in. And the first place they'd look would be the Quonset hut.

She moved away from the gap, then raced back to the fence, careful not to touch it this time, unsure of how the alarm was triggered. The two guards must have not been too concerned, since it had taken them so long to respond. Maybe lulled by previous false alarms, they had waited until whatever television pro-gram or movie they were watching had ended.

She reached the gap and paused to listen again. She didn't hear anything, but the silence didn't soothe her. The two guards were still around, she was sure. And if she couldn't hear them, neither could Dane.

She drew her weapon and, heart pounding painfully, she slipped through the gap in the fence and crept toward the Quonset. She was almost to the hut when bright lights flooded the backyard. She didn't hesitate, but dove into the shadows between the back of the Quonset and the fence. She crouched there, panting and trying to control her shaking. Shouts rose from someone, then a sound of scuffling inside the hut. The noise was so close she thought she could have reached out and touched whoever was involved.

Then she heard a familiar voice, deep and forceful, full of anger and pain. Her heart clenched. Dane! The voices receded toward the front of the hut. She moved to the side and looked down the long length of the Quonset. After an agonizing interval, two men crossed the yard, Dane between them. His body was limp, and they struggled to drag him. Was he only unconscious—or dead?

She should go back through the fence now. She should run to the truck and drive back to the highway, to Ranger Brigade headquarters, where she could summon help. But even as she thought this, a third man emerged from the guesthouse and moved toward the fence, where he replaced the log Dane had removed, blocking her exit. She could do nothing but sit and wait, helpless, as Dane receded from sight.

DANE'S HEAD THROBBED where the stockier of the two guards had cold-cocked him. The rest of him probably hurt, too, considering his arms were bound tightly behind his back and he could feel a bruise swelling on his face. But the pain in his head trumped them all. The guy had fists like iron.

He opened his eyes enough to determine he was lying on his side in a room with white Berber carpet and dark paneling. Then he closed them again, pretending to be unconscious, hoping to learn more about his possible fate.

"If we cut his throat and dump the body, the boss never has to know." The man who spoke had an accent—Texas, maybe.

"What happens when somebody finds the body and it ends up on the news?" another man, with a higher pitched voice, asked.

"So what?" a third man asked. "He won't know it had anything to do with us."

"He'll know."

"And we'll be lucky if he doesn't shoot us and dump our bodies," Texas said.

"Not necessarily." High Voice walked over and nudged Dane with the toe of his boot. "You know who this is, don't you? It's Dane Trask. Terrell will be so happy we've got him, he'll probably give us a bonus."

"If he's not happy, I'm blaming it all on you two," the third man said. "I wasn't even awake when this was going down. You two were supposed to be on duty, instead of on your duffs in front of the TV."

"You're always asleep," Texas said. "Even when you're supposed to be awake."

"Shut up," High Voice snapped. He moved away from Dane, but seconds later, a shower of ice-cold water jolted him, followed by laughter.

"Wake up." High Voice nudged him with his boot again.

Dane glared up at the man but said nothing.

"Mr. Terrell is not going to be happy to see you," High Voice said.

The feeling is mutual, Dane thought.

"We took your phone," Texas said. "We smashed it good. You won't be sharing those pictures you took with anyone."

"Hey, did you know there's a big reward for your capture?" the third man said. He was wiry and balding, corded muscles standing out on his arms. "Think we'll be eligible for the cash?"

The others laughed, as if this was the funniest thing they'd heard in months. Dane waited, silent. Maybe it was his military training on how to deal with interrogations, or maybe just a reluctance to talk to these criminals. He closed his eyes, his head throbbing.

Someone—probably High Voice—kicked him in the ribs. Hard. Dane gritted his teeth to keep from crying out. "Wake up," High Voice said. "It's almost morning. Mr. Terrell is an early riser. He'll want to see you."

You said he won't be happy to see me, Dane thought. *Make up your mind.*

"How did you get here?" High Voice asked. "I know you didn't hike all the way over here from the national park."

Dane merely looked at him.

"Maybe he flew," Texas said.

"Or maybe he had help," the third man said.

Dane's heart lurched, though he kept his expression impassive. He couldn't let these three find Faith.

"Did you see any sign of anyone else out there?" Texas asked.

"No. The ground's too dry for tracks—and it's dark anyway. I thought I heard some rustling in the woods, but it turned out to be a squirrel or something. I saw it run up a tree. I put the post back in the fence and reset the alarm."

"Maybe the squirrel ran because something else—or someone else—disturbed it," Texas said. "Did you think of that? You should have walked back and looked."

The third man frowned. "There wasn't anybody back there," he said. "But if it'll make you happy, I'll go look." He grasped the arms of his chair and started to push himself up.

"I don't need help to outsmart you three," Dane said, disdain in every word. "I'd been in that Quonset hut twenty minutes before you even bothered to see what had tripped your alarm. Terrell is going to be thrilled to hear about that. You'll be lucky if you can find a job guarding sheep after this."

This earned him another blow to the ribs and a barrage of curses. But, for the moment, they had forgotten about Faith.

Someone's phone rang. The third man unclipped a smartphone from his belt and answered it. "Uh-huh… Uh-huh… Yes, sir… Yes, sir." He ended the call and looked at the others. "Mr. Terrell is up. He got the message I left for him and he wants to see Trask."

Texas hauled Dane to his feet. "Come on," he said. "You're finally going to get what's coming to you."

FAITH WAITED UNTIL she was sure the man was gone, then carefully emerged from her hiding place. She didn't think her pursuer had done much more than set the log Dane had removed back in place. She could probably shift it and get into the compound that way. She dismissed the idea. Rather than stepping through the gap in the fence and risking triggering the alarm again, she decided to approach the house from the front. She had to find out where Dane was being held, and if he was all right. Calling for help might be the wiser choice, but by the time that help arrived, Dane might be dead. If she could pinpoint his location, she could at least get help to him that much sooner.

Charles Terrell's home presented an imposing façade from the street, in a mix of adobe-and-log architecture that reminded Faith of the clay and Lincoln Logs' structures she and her brothers had built as children. She supposed Terrell, or maybe his decorator wife, thought of this as Western Chic or Southwest Modern, or some other hip label.

One thing was for sure—the place was big. Two stories tall, it sprawled almost the whole width of the large lot, with towers and parapets, covered and uncovered porches and patios, and various attached and unattached outbuildings. A sweeping circular drive curved in front of the house, with two dark SUVs parked out front. Though it was only a little after six in the morning, lights glowed in several of the windows. Was Dane in one of those rooms?

She avoided the driveway and kept to a thin belt of trees along the property line, which had probably been left as a privacy screen from the neighbors. In the early darkness, the brush provided enough cover for Faith to move closer to the house. When she was even with the two parked vehicles, she stopped and waited. What now?

No one moved outside the house. She spotted a couple of cameras focused on the driveway, but none on the sides. The windows and doors were probably alarmed. If she waited until someone emerged from the house, could she possibly slip in when they went back inside?

She dismissed the idea—way too dangerous. She wasn't going to be able to help Dane if she got caught. Disappointed, but driven by a new sense of urgency, she turned and began creeping back toward the road. She'd run all the way to the truck and drive as fast as she could to Ranger headquarters. Dane was tough. He would hang on.

She was halfway to the street when the sound of a slamming door made her freeze. She turned to see two men—possibly the same two she had spotted earlier—once more dragging Dane between them. As they wrestled him into one of the SUVs, Charles Terrell emerged from the house and stood on the porch, hands on his hips. He said something that she couldn't make out and one of the men with Dane answered.

Dane said something, too, which earned him a punch to the side of the head. His hands were tied behind his back and his ankles were bound. He looked rough, as if they had beaten him. Dirt or dried blood smeared his face.

Faith looked away and focused on Terrell. Dressed in jeans and a button-down shirt with the sleeves rolled up, he looked like an average middle-aged executive on a Saturday morning, though his expression was anything but relaxed. He spoke again, and the two guards began wrestling Dane into the back of the SUV. A chill swept over Faith. They were taking him out to kill him. They would dump his body somewhere on public land, the way they had dumped other people who had gotten in their way—the reporter, Roy Holliday, and Larry Keplar. By the time she summoned help, it would be too late. They'd only be able to search for Dane's body.

She eased the Glock from its holster and took aim. The first shot punctured the rear tire of the SUV. Both guards shouted and let go of Dane, who hit the ground hard, like a rug that had suddenly been dropped. Faith fired again, this time at the wall behind Terrell. A window shattered and he dove to the porch floor, hands over his head, shouting at the guards to do something.

The two men took cover behind the vehicle and began firing in her direction. Their shots were wild; they hadn't yet figured out where she was. She slipped through the brush, moving closer to the house, trying for stealth, but the sky was growing lighter, reducing her cover. Bullets struck near her. She stopped and, from behind the cover of a large rock, she fired toward Terrell again. He was still cowering on the porch, apparently too paralyzed by fear to go into the house, out of harm's way.

She checked the SUV again. Dane had rolled under the vehicle, so he was safe, at least. One man still fired in her general direction, but the other had moved out and was headed toward her.

Faith fired, clipping his shoulder. "Stop right there!" she shouted. "I've got my gun aimed on Terrell and I will shoot to kill if you come any closer." To prove her point, she shot into the porch floorboards, inches from Terrell's head. He screamed profanities as she shoved another clip into the Glock.

"Untie Trask," she called.

No one moved.

"Untie him," she shouted and then shot out the window on the other side of Terrell.

"Do as she says!" Terrell shouted.

The taller of the two guards—the one who wasn't gripping his bleeding shoulder—took a knife from his pocket and cut Dane free.

"You two move into the house," she called. "Terrell stays out here."

Again, no one moved. This time, she aimed a little closer to Terrell, who lay prone, not even trying to get away.

The guards moved then, Terrell shouting at them. Dane stumbled toward the woods, heading not for her, but for a spot closer to the road. Faith fired at the house again and more glass shattered. Then she took off running, praying Dane would be strong enough to follow.

DANE IGNORED THE pain in his ribs and arms and ran, catching up with Faith at the rear corner of the property. "How do we get to the truck?" she asked.

"This way."

The trek took longer than he would have liked, since they were forced to stick to cover. Once, he thought he spotted the second dark SUV cruising down the street, Texas in the passenger seat, scanning the surroundings for any sign of them.

He estimated it took almost an hour to make a trip that had taken less than twenty minutes only a few hours before. They piled into the FJ and Faith started the engine and sped forward, jouncing over the rough ground until he cried out from the pain in his ribs. She immediately took her foot off the gas and turned to him, her face stricken. "Are you hurt? I should have asked before."

"Keep going," he said through gritted teeth. "We have to get out of here."

She didn't argue, and started forward again, though a little more slowly this time, until they reached the highway, where she floored the gas pedal. Without his asking, she took the back way to the remote pull-off where they had hidden the FJ before. She parked and they got out. He waited while she arranged branches to cover the vehicle, then she turned to him. "Can you make the hike to the cave?" she asked, scanning him with a worried expression.

"I don't have any choice," he said, and turned and began walking, or rather, limping, away from the truck.

By the time they reached the cave, he was gritting his teeth to keep from groaning with every step, and sweating heavily. But Faith had enough sense to leave him be. She followed along behind, the heavy pack on her back. At one point, they spotted a lone fly fisherman on the river, and had to retreat to cover and wait until he had moved on before they continued. Faith handed Dane a water bottle and he drained it, but refused the protein bar she offered, half sick from the adrenaline surge of the past few hours.

The sun was high in the sky before they reached the welcome dimness of the cave. He stumbled inside and crawled to his sleeping bag, and lay on his back, eyes closed, utterly exhausted. Light flickered behind his eyes as Faith lit the lantern. She moved around the space, pouring water and taking items from the pack. Then she knelt beside him, her touch light on his arm. "Are you okay?" she asked.

"I will be." He started to sit up, but she pushed him down. "I'm going to wipe the dried blood from your face and then I'm going to check that you don't have any broken bones."

"Just leave me alone to rest," he said, but without any heat behind the words.

She ignored him and began dabbing at his face with a wet cloth. The fabric brushed against his beard, bringing with it the scent of antiseptic and soap. She took his hand in hers and examined the fingers, then felt up his arm. He winced when she touched a bruise.

"Sorry," she said. "You're going to have to take off this shirt."

She helped him sit up, and he eased off the shirt, wincing as he did so. She brought the lamp closer and scowled at the purpling marks on his torso. "What did they do to you?" she asked.

"They got in a few good kicks," he admitted.

"You could have broken ribs." Not waiting for an answer, she began running her hands lightly up and down his sides. The pain receded somewhat as he registered the sensation of her silken touch along sensitive nerve endings. When she skimmed her hands over his abdomen, he felt it in his groin and flinched. "Does that hurt?" she asked.

"Not exactly."

She sent him a questioning look, and her touch became firmer, the pain returning. He grunted. So much for a sensual moment.

At last, she sat back. "Any sharp pain when you breathe?" she asked.

"No. It pretty much hurts all the time."

"I can't be certain, but I don't think anything is broken—just badly bruised. You must have strong bones."

She started to move away but he grabbed her wrist. "Why did you do that?" he asked.

"Do what?"

"Challenge them that way. Shoot at them. There

were three of them and one of you. They could have easily overwhelmed and killed you." Thinking about it now made his head swim.

"I had the element of surprise in my favor." She eased out of his grip, but kept one hand resting lightly on his forearm. "Terrell is a coward. He's not used to being vulnerable, and his bodyguards have been trained to do what he says."

She couldn't have known that. She had taken a huge risk. "You were supposed to go back to the truck and wait to meet up with me," he said.

She shook her head. "I saw them take you. I couldn't just leave you." Her eyes met his, steady and full of accusation. "You wouldn't have left me."

No, he wouldn't have. Why did he believe she should have behaved differently? Was it because she was a woman? Or because he thought her life was more important than his? The idea startled him. He'd never been a fatalist. "I'm not sorry you didn't go," he said. "I'm only saying you were reckless. That isn't like you."

"Maybe some of you is rubbing off on me." She looked away. "Does it hurt anywhere else?"

"I'm cold," he said, which was true, but when she turned to look for a blanket, he tugged her hand. "Lie down here beside me. We can keep each other warm."

He fully expected her to protest. Despite the kiss they had shared, he wasn't sure how she felt about him. Yes, she had risked her life to save him, but as a law enforcement officer, she would have likely done the same for anyone—even Terrell.

"All right," she said, and eased herself next to him on top of the sleeping bag.

"It's okay." He slid his arm beneath her head. "You can move closer."

She fit against him snugly, her warmth seeping into him. She nestled her head in the hollow of his shoulder and rested her hand, palm down, in the center of his chest. He covered her hand with his own. "Tell me what happened," she said. "Did you get inside the Quonset hut? What did you find?"

"I cut a hole in the side first, to look in. There were a lot of empty metal shelves, and a big tractor-trailer. I unzipped the cover at the rear of the hut and went in. The back of the trailer was open and you were right— Terrell is using his property to store the drugs. There were thousands of heroin bricks in there, packed in barrels labeled as fertilizer."

"Did they catch you in the trailer?"

"Yes. Inside the truck, I didn't hear them coming."

"I heard them, and saw them, but I didn't have any way of warning you. I overheard them talking about a silent alarm on the fence that tipped them off, but apparently they've had a lot of false alarms before, from wildlife, so they hadn't been in any hurry checking this one out."

"When no one came out right after I breached the fence, I thought I was in the clear," he said. He turned his head, his nose almost touching her cheek. "You were supposed to whistle to warn me."

"It was too late. All that would have done is let them know I was there."

"They didn't know you were there. At one point, they were speculating on whether I was alone or with someone, and I distracted them."

"How did you do that?"

"With my usual charm."

Dane felt rather than saw her lips curve into a smile. She settled more firmly against him, though she was still wearing her body armor, its stiffness detracting somewhat from the moment. "I saw them dragging you toward the house," she said. "What happened after that?"

"They waited until Terrell summoned them, then dragged me up to the house. Apparently, he's an early riser. I think he's at the house by himself. Either that, or his wife is willing to look the other way while he breaks the law. He didn't seem anxious to hide any of his activities."

"They were going to kill you." Her voice was flat, not asking a question.

"Yes. They planned to dump my body on public land somewhere remote, where it wouldn't be found for a very long time."

"I had to stop them," Faith said.

"You could have killed Terrell. That would have stopped them."

She blew out a long breath. "I'm sworn to uphold the law, not break it. It's up to the courts to pass sentence on Charles Terrell, not me."

"I respect you for that." He didn't think he would have done the same in her shoes, but maybe he would have. Killing someone in self-defense or in the midst of a battle was a long way from shooting a man—even a man like Terrell—in cold blood. He tightened his arm around her shoulder. "You were pretty amazing out there," he said.

"I was desperate." She spoke softly, her lips against his chest. "I think I realized a little of what you've been going through these past two months."

He shifted to roll toward her, ignoring the pain in his side as he focused on her. She tilted her head up to him, her lips full and slightly parted, her pupils dark and dilated with need. He kissed her gently, the barest brush of his lips against hers, ready to pull back if she protested. But instead of objecting, Faith snaked her hand up to press the back of his head, urging him closer, surging up to meet him with an urgency that stirred him.

He kissed her lips for a long time, then pulled away to kiss her closed eyelids and the gently beating pulse at her temple. Her fingers fluttered over his skin in tickling, teasing caresses. Breathing hard, he grasped her wrists. "How far do you want to go with this?" he asked.

Her smile held heat and promise. "How far are you able to take me?" she whispered, the rough desire in her voice driving his lust up another notch.

Chapter Fourteen

Faith had given Dane the answer he wanted, and he wasn't going to waste any more time. "We have to get rid of this vest," he said. He slid his hand under Faith's shirt and knocked at the hard carapace around her torso.

She sat and unbuttoned the khaki uniform shirt, then ripped open the hook-and-loop tape fastening the body armor in place. The next layer was a soft knit camisole, the dark areolas of her breasts showing through the thin fabric, a teasing peep show that made it harder for him to breathe.

She didn't stop with the armor, but stripped off completely, until she was naked, chill bumps dancing across her pink-and-white skin, her nipples tight buds crowning her small, round breasts. He felt greedy, staring at her, taking her in. She eased down beside him and propped her head on her elbow to watch him. "Your turn," she said.

Dane managed to work his way out of his hiking pants and socks. He wasn't wearing any underwear, having discarded it weeks ago as one less thing to wash. His erection sprang free as he pulled down the pants, and she smiled, her cheeks flushed bright pink, eyes sparkling.

When he lay down again, she slid over to him then on top of him, her thighs straddling his hips, her palms sliding across the muscles of his chest. He shaped his own hands to her hips, then up to her waist, then up still farther to cup her breasts. "Are you sure you're up to this?" she asked, teasing.

"I don't know, what do you think?" He rocked against her, nudging her with his erection.

HE WAS READY, all right, Faith thought. And so was she. She'd had every intention of conducting a serious, professional examination of his bruised ribs, but once she had realized he was all right, she had been distracted by his taut muscles and smooth skin.

Everything about Dane Trask fascinated her, from his athletic body to his fierce determination and maddening assumption that whatever action he decided to take was the right thing to do. He was smart, but also incredibly stubborn, both unwilling to rely on or be a burden to anyone else, yet also selfish, insisting on always doing things his way. He was a maddening collection of positive and negative traits and he had cast a spell on her she didn't want to break.

"Are you ready?" he asked, nudging her again.

"Maybe." She leaned toward him and he took one nipple in his mouth, smiling against her when she gave a cry of delight. She shifted so that she was sitting farther back, his erection cradled against her, his eyes glazing over as she stroked him with her hand. She liked this, having him somewhat at her mercy. It evened the odds a little, and paid him back for his caveman machismo when they'd first met.

"There's a condom in the first-aid kit in the pack," he said, breaking through the fog of desire. "More than one, probably."

"I thought you came out here alone, intending to stay that way," she said. "What are you doing with condoms?"

"They can come in handy for a lot of things."

Right now Faith was most interested in the thing condoms were designed for. She slid off him and retrieved the pack and the first-aid kit inside, aware of his eyes on her. Away from his warmth, the cave was cold, so she grabbed up the blanket from where he had slept the night before and brought it and the condom to him. "You put it on," he said when she tried to hand it to him.

She tore open the packet, then took him in her hand, unable to resist a few strokes before he stilled her wrists. "Careful," he said, his voice a low growl that settled in the pit of her stomach. Yes, she had better be careful with this man. He had a way of getting to her that she couldn't decide if she liked or not.

But right now, she definitely liked the way he made her feel. She lay back beside him and he leaned over to kiss her deeply, lips and tongue and hands silencing whatever feeble protest was left in her brain.

He nudged at her hips. "I liked it when you were

on top," he said. "I think I'm getting used to you being in charge."

She laughed, but slid onto him once more and settled over him. Her laughter died as he filled her, and she closed her eyes as they began to move together, pleasure building, desire growing. His arms wrapped around her as he arced to meet her, and she felt so treasured, overwhelmed by emotion. She shifted to bring him closer still. Deeper.

He slid his hand between them to caress her and, within moments, his skilled touch took her over the edge. She cried out as he thrust harder, and she rode him to his completion, then kissed him deeply, her body pressed to his, his arms holding her tight against him.

It was a long time before they slid apart, and longer still before they spoke. He smoothed her hair and tucked one lock behind her ear. "I'm sorry about the way you ended up here," he said. "But I'm not sorry you're here now."

"No, I'm not sorry." She raised her head up so she could see his face. "What are we going to do about Terrell?"

He let out a long breath and pain returned to his eyes. "We'll talk about it later," he said. "Right now, we need to sleep."

Faith lay down and closed her eyes, and he pulled the blanket up around them, reaching over her to switch off the lantern. Warmth seeped into her and her breathing slowed in rhythm with his own. She laced her fingers with Dane's and let herself relax.

Tomorrow she'd think about the danger they were in. Tomorrow she would figure out how to deal with her fear.

"YOU'RE ABSOLUTELY SURE Dane Trask is the man who attacked you?" Carmen surveyed the broken glass littering the front porch of the oversize adobe-and-log mansion Charles Terrell had summoned them to. Several bullet holes marked the cedar frames around the windows, and the body of the SUV that sat, one tire flat and the windshield shattered, in front of the house.

"He came here in the middle of the night and threatened me and my employees." Terrell gestured to the two men who sat in folding chairs on the porch, their eyes downcast, big hands resting loosely in their laps. A third man had been transported by ambulance with a gunshot wound in his shoulder.

"How do you know it was Dane Trask?" Hud asked. The commander had delegated him and Carmen to respond to this call, which technically was out of their jurisdiction. But at the mention of Dane Trask, the county sheriff had agreed the Ranger Brigade should handle it.

"Because he said so. And because the man worked for me for six years and I recognized him. I didn't recognize the woman who was with him, though."

The words ignited Carmen. "What woman? What did she look like?"

Terrell shook his head. "I didn't get a good look

at her, but she did all the shooting." He gestured at the broken glass. "She said she was going to kill me."

Hud met Carmen's gaze behind Terrell's back. Then he bent to examine one of the bullet holes in the window frame. "I can see part of the bullet in there," he said. "It could be a .40-caliber S&W."

The Glocks most of the Ranger Brigade carried used that type of ammunition. It didn't mean the woman Terrell had seen was Faith, but it was the closest they had come to any sighting of her since she had disappeared three days ago. "Tell us again everything that happened," Carmen said.

Terrell crossed his arms over his chest. "I was in the kitchen, drinking my first cup of coffee and reviewing some work emails, when I heard a pounding on the front door. I looked out and saw Dane Trask on the doorstep. Of course, I was stunned to see him, but glad, too. He's been missing so long. I opened the door and the next thing I knew he was pointing a gun at me. I yelled for help and my men came running."

"Where was the woman when this was happening?" Hud asked.

"She was standing back, in the shadows. When the others came running, she started shooting. She was screaming and shooting out windows like a wild woman."

"I don't understand," Carmen said. "What did Trask and this woman want? Did they say why they were here?"

"They wanted to kill me."

"But they didn't kill you." Carmen surveyed the

damage again. "She fired a lot of shots, and from what you say, she was quite close, but she didn't kill you."

"I guess I'm lucky she was such a poor shot," he said.

Faith was not a poor shot. Carmen had been at the shooting range with her. The deputy had a steady hand and better aim than many with the handgun. She wouldn't have missed if she had been aiming at a man standing still on his front porch. "Where was she standing when this happened?"

"Out there." He motioned toward the side of the house.

"So, Dane Trask was on the front porch with you, and the woman was out there, shooting?"

"Yes."

"What did Dane do while she was shooting?" Carmen asked. She was trying to picture the scene, but failing.

"He…he hid behind the SUV." Terrell nodded at the vehicle with the shattered window and the flat tire.

"So she shot up the car and your house, and wounded your employee, then they just left?" Hud asked.

"Yes."

"Why did they leave?" Carmen asked.

Terrell glared at her. "I don't know. But they're not here, so they obviously left."

Hud gestured to the cameras at either end of the front porch. "Lucky you have these security cameras. We should be able to get the whole scene from your recordings."

Terrell licked his lips. "Unfortunately, those cameras aren't working right now. I haven't gotten around to hooking them up."

Hud nodded. "What time was it when Trask knocked on your door?"

"It was early. A little after six o'clock."

Hud made a show of looking at his watch. "It's almost noon now. Why did you wait so long to call us?"

"I sent Pete and Ryan out to look for Trask and his accomplice. I thought it was important to try to track them down."

"It's our job to track them down. Or the sheriff's."

"The Ranger Brigade is handling the search for Dane Trask, aren't they?" Terrell said. "I thought you would appreciate knowing he was here."

"What did you do in the almost six hours between when this happened and now?" Hud asked.

"I had a stiff drink and another cup of coffee. I tried to persuade Mason to go to the hospital, but he preferred to wait here with me."

When Carmen and Hud arrived, Mason had stopped bleeding and had the wound bandaged and in a sling. Someone at this house—probably not Terrell—knew something about wound care. "Six hours is a long time to wait," she said, waiting for more explanation from Terrell.

"I was in shock," Terrell said. "I lost track of time."

"We'll look around," Hud said. "See if we find anything helpful." He moved away from the porch, eyes on the ground, toward the general area Terrell had indicated Trask's companion had fired from.

"Can you tell me anything more about this woman who was with Trask?" Carmen asked. "Was she short? Tall? Fair or dark?"

"It was dark. I was terrified. I can't tell you anything."

"But you're sure it was a woman?"

"Yes. She had a woman's voice. And she was very concerned about protecting Trask."

"Protecting him from what?"

"I don't know that, either. Now, if you'll excuse me, I have things to do." Not waiting for an answer, he turned and went back into the house.

Carmen went to the door and knocked. "Mr. Terrell, I haven't finished talking to you," she said. Silence. She tried the knob, but the door was locked.

"Officer Redhorse, come here a minute," Hud called.

A thin line of scrub grew between the house and a utility easement. Hud squatted next to a red marker he had placed. He pointed into the grass beside the marker. "Spent shell from a .40 S&W," he said. "It's the same brand we use." He stood. "There's a lot of brush beat down, as if someone crouched here for a while. And I found this." He indicated a second marker, this one on the end of a branch of scrub oak.

Carmen stared at the two strands of dark, curly hair snagged on the end of the branch. "Faith's hair is that color," she said. She turned to Hud. "But why would Faith be shooting out windows at Charles Terrell's home? It doesn't make sense."

"It doesn't make sense that Terrell has security cameras but no recordings," Hud said. "Or that he has three bodyguards on the premises at six in the morning."

"Maybe he's had threats made against him," Carmen suggested. "Or he's paranoid about being attacked."

"All the more reasons to have those cameras turned on."

"Or, he turned them off so we wouldn't see what really happened with Trask and this mysterious woman," Carmen said. "Or maybe he's lying about the woman. Maybe it was just Trask."

"Someone was shooting from here," Hud said. "Someone with dark, curly hair. Like Faith."

Carmen frowned at the hairs, fine as spider's silk, hanging limp from the branch. "We'll get Forensics out here. Meanwhile, let's take a look around."

She led the way along the line of brush, toward a large, double gate that opened onto a fenced-off area behind the house. She peered over the fence, at a small cottage that might have been a guesthouse, and beyond it, at the very back corner of the property, a large canvas Quonset hut.

One of the bodyguards—the shorter of the two, Ryan—moved toward her. "You can't come back here," he said.

"Why not?" Hud asked.

"Because it's private property."

"What's in the Quonset hut?" Hud nodded toward the large canvas-sided structure.

"Mr. Terrell collects sports cars. He keeps them back there."

"Not in the garage?" Hud looked toward the three-car garage on the other side of the house.

"He has a large collection."

"What happened here today?" Carmen asked. "What do you remember?"

"Mr. Terrell already told you everything." The man's expression was sullen. He didn't look stupid, just stubborn. And he definitely didn't like being questioned by cops.

"You may have noticed something he didn't see," Carmen said. "It's often helpful to get accounts from several different witnesses."

"I have work to do. I don't have time to talk to you." He turned away.

"We can ask you to come to Ranger Brigade headquarters with us, if you'd rather talk there," Hud said.

Ryan stopped and turned back to them. "It happened like Mr. Terrell said," he said. "Someone knocked on the door. Mr. Terrell went to answer it. A few minutes later, he yelled for help. Pete and Mason and I went running. We saw Dane Trask standing in front of Mr. Terrell. He was yelling something—I couldn't make out what he was saying. Then a woman screamed at us and started shooting out windows.

Mason went down and after that all hell broke loose." He shrugged. "It was wild, but it was over with pretty fast."

"What happened after that?" Hud asked.

"I bandaged up Mason. Mr. Terrell tried to get him to go to the hospital, but he didn't want to. Then Pete and I took a car out to look for Trask and the woman. But we didn't find them."

"Why didn't you answer the knock on the door?" Hud asked.

"It's Mr. Terrell's house."

"But you're his bodyguard, aren't you?" Hud asked. "I would think checking to see who is at the door would be part of your duties."

"I don't know what you're talking about. Is that all?"

A long moment of pained silence followed then Hud said, "Sure. If we have more questions, we'll talk to you later."

He left and Carmen and Hud walked back toward the front of the property. "Should we talk to Pete?" she asked.

"Later. Though I don't think we're going to get anything else out of them." He stopped and turned back to survey the house. "Faith never struck me as the type to go on a wild shooting spree," he said.

"No," Carmen agreed.

"Maybe it's Stockholm syndrome."

"Maybe." Was it possible that Dane Trask *had* kidnapped Faith, and in three days' time managed to

make her…what—fall in love with him? Lose her
mind to the point where she shot out windows and
made wild demands of a businessman Trask used to
work for? "We need to find her," she said. "And Trask.
Before someone else gets hurt."

Chapter Fifteen

Over a late lunch of canned chicken and grated cheese over pasta, Dane and Faith discussed their next move. "I'm supposed to meet my friend for supplies this afternoon," he said. "I'll ask him what he's heard."

"Who is your friend?" she asked.

"He's a fellow ranger—an Army Ranger. We served together in Afghanistan. We reconnected when he came into Welcome Home Warriors. After I started hiding out here, he left some supplies with a note, saying he'd bring me anything I needed—he'd be in that same spot in a week's time to meet me."

"You didn't suspect a trap?"

"I did. But I made sure I was at the rendezvous point before he came. I didn't see anything suspicious and he came alone. And I was pretty sure he wouldn't betray me."

"How could you be sure? Because he was in the Army Rangers with you?"

"Yes. And because he owed me."

Faith waited, not pressing him to say more. He liked that about her. She wasn't pushy or needy, or any of the things that made him pull away from people.

"After he got out of the service, he was doing a lot of drugs," he said. "I helped him get the help he needed to quit." He shrugged. "It wasn't a big deal to me, but it was to him. So he helps me. I wouldn't be doing half so well if he didn't."

"He agrees with what you're doing, then."

"I didn't say that. But he trusts me to make my own decisions."

Dane's eyes met hers, but she didn't flinch. "When your friend decided to be on drugs, that was a wrong decision," she said.

"Proving what, exactly?" he asked.

"Sometimes people make the wrong decisions. They need a friend to turn them around."

Was she saying she was the friend who was going to turn him around? He did see things differently since he had dragged her into this mess. She made him stop and think—and when she did something rash herself, like shooting out windows at Charles Terrell's place and charging in like a one-woman cavalry to save him, it made him question all of his own impulsive decisions.

He leaned forward and kissed her—a quick brush of lips against her cheek.

"What was that for?" she asked.

"Because I wanted to." He grinned. "I'm impulsive that way."

She laughed. A sound that made his chest feel tight—thrilled and a little afraid at the same time, like when he was a kid and sat poised for long seconds at the top of a roller coaster. She set aside her plate and wiped her fingers on a paper napkin. "How is Terrell going to explain his shot-up SUV and shattered windows?" she asked. "Not to mention the wounded guard? Do you think he'll call the sheriff's office and report an attack?"

"He might," Dane said. "It would be one more thing he can blame on me."

"I think it's time to admit we're in over our heads and go to the Rangers for help."

He looked away. "But can they really help?"

"It's not just your word against Terrell's now," she said. "You've got me. The Rangers and the sheriff and everyone else in law enforcement aren't going to ignore a fellow officer."

She felt a stab of pain as his shoulders slumped. He looked ten years older and utterly exhausted. "One thing's for sure. Terrell is going to be gunning hard for me now—for both of us."

"He doesn't know who I am," she said, though how could she be sure of that?

"He'll figure it out." He stood and began gathering up the remains of their meal. "Let's sleep on it, then let me talk to my friend this afternoon."

"All right." If nothing else, that would give them one more night together, a night where she didn't have to think about all the ways the world might tear them apart.

"WE WON'T HAVE the test results back from the hair we found at Terrell's place for a few more days, but for now we're operating on the assumption that the woman with Dane Trask is Faith Martin." Commander

Sanderlin addressed the gathered Ranger Brigade officers Saturday afternoon, his expression grim. "We don't know why she's with him or what they were trying to accomplish at Terrell's house, but you're to proceed with the idea that they are armed and dangerous."

"We don't know what really happened at Terrell's home this morning," Hud said. "His story doesn't match up with what little evidence we were able to gather."

"It's possible the shots the woman with him fired were defensive, not offensive," Carmen said.

"It's possible," Sanderlin said. "We won't know until we find these two and capture them."

"Terrell is hiding something," Hud said. "I think he was lying about the security cameras not being on."

"Again, we can only proceed on the basis of what he's told us." The commander glanced at the notes in front of him. "Terrell's home is eight miles from the park boundary. While it's possible Martin and Trask walked that far, I think it's more likely they have a vehicle, possibly stolen." He turned to Lieutenant Dance. "What did you find out?"

"I came up with reports of three stolen vehicles in the area, but all of them are in Montrose. None in the park."

"I think I know what they might be driving."

Everyone shifted to stare at Jason Beck, who flushed. "This morning when I retrieved the keys for my cruiser, I noticed the slot for the old FJ was empty." He shrugged. "It was just something I noted in passing. I didn't think much of it. But now I wonder."

"Faith would have known about the spare cruiser,"

Reynolds said. "And she'd have an entry code for the building."

"Beck, go see if the FJ is on the lot," Sanderlin said.

"Yes, sir."

Beck left and Sanderlin returned to his notes. "We've had APBs out on Martin and Trask. We're now emphasizing that they are probably traveling together. We're also sending additional publicity to the media, and posting information in the national park."

Carmen's heart sank. What would Faith think when she saw her image on what was, effectively, a Wanted poster? Had a dedicated officer lost all sense of duty over a reckless man? Carmen had always heard that love could make people do strange things, but she couldn't believe it of Faith. Women didn't make it this far in law enforcement by coloring outside the lines.

Sanderlin reviewed their duty assignments for the day.

Beck returned to the room. "The FJ is gone," he said.

"Then we can find it," Sanderlin said.

"The GPS tracker." Hud sat straighter. "You're sure there's one on that old thing?"

"All of our vehicles are equipped with tracking devices," Sanderlin said. "In case an officer gets stranded in the middle of nowhere, or one of the vehicles gets stolen."

Hud shoved back his chair, more animated than Carmen had seen him all morning. "I'll get right on it."

"Let's hope Faith and Trask are with the vehicle," Dance said.

"And let's hope neither one of them does anything stupid," Carmen muttered as she followed the others from the room. Like the rest of them, she'd be out looking for Faith today. She hoped she found her fellow officer first, so she could question her privately, and ask what had happened with Trask to take her life so far off course.

DANE STARED AT the flyer Steve Betcher handed him when they met Saturday afternoon. Faith, looking particularly stern in her Ranger Brigade uniform, her hair pulled back into a tight bun, stared out from a color photograph next to a picture of him, taken on a hike with Audra last year. In the photograph, he was clean-shaved and grinning, posed at an overlook along the canyon rim.

The flyer proclaimed in bold black type:

WANTED!

Law enforcement seeks information about the whereabouts of these two people. If you see them, DO NOT APPROACH. They may be armed and dangerous. Contact a park ranger or the nearest law enforcement agency immediately.

There followed a description of Faith and then Dane.

"I stole that off a bulletin board by the park visitor center," Betcher said. "One of the Ranger Brigade officers had just tacked it up."

Dane folded the flyer and tucked it into his pocket.

"Leave it to you to hook up with a good-looking woman out here in the middle of nowhere," Betcher said. "But what's the 'armed and dangerous' bit?"

"It's all a misunderstanding," Dane said.

"And I don't need to know the details. Gotcha." Betcher handed over a cloth tote. "Fresh groceries and the local and Denver papers," he said. "Though I don't think there's anything about you—or your new girlfriend—in there."

"Thanks." Dane took the bag. "I promise you, I haven't done anything illegal—or dangerous."

"I know." Betcher smiled. "You only did what you had to do. It's how we roll." He clapped Dane on the shoulder. "One day, I'm going to want to hear all the details. In the meantime, see you Wednesday."

Dane nodded. Wednesday seemed a long time away. He hoped he and Faith were still free—and still alive—by then.

He returned to the cave by a different route from the one he had traveled on his way to meet Betcher— a habit he had established early in his exile. A worn path might lead a casual hiker to follow the trail to his hideout, and a routine made it easier for someone looking for him to spot him. His return journey took him past the pullout where he and Faith had stashed the FJ when they'd returned to the park this morning. He gave the area a wide berth, but glanced over to check that the vehicle was still there.

It wasn't. That was evident right away. Brush had been hacked away and pulled back, the grass around the area trampled. Seeing this, he quickened his pace, retreating far from the road and going several miles out of the way to avoid anyone who might be hunting for him in the area.

Instead of descending into the canyon via a trail, he made a treacherous climb down the rock wall, the tote bag of supplies slung around his shoulders in a makeshift backpack. When he made it to the river, he waited another hour, watching the route to the cave for any sign of another person. Satisfied their hideout hadn't yet been discovered, he carefully made his way there.

The cave was dark when he arrived, and silent. A chill swept over him as he moved further into the interior, and his heart pounded hard as he listened for some indication that he wasn't alone. "Faith?" he whispered. Then, a little louder. "Faith? It's me—Dane."

A light flickered at the far end of the cave, and Faith stepped out. "I was worried when you stayed away so long," she said. "I heard someone coming and wasn't sure it was you."

"Good idea." He pulled her close, the feel of her pressed against him calming. "I'm certain I wasn't followed. We're okay."

"What took you so long?" she asked as he set the tote bag on the floor.

"We've got some trouble," he said. "The FJ is gone."

"Gone?"

"I swung by where we parked it and the brush is all hacked away and the vehicle isn't there."

"The Rangers must have found it," she said.

"Someone noticed it was missing and went looking for it." She shook her head. "It doesn't really matter. They can't track us to the cave from there."

"They've got a tracking dog, don't they?" he asked. "It might get them close." He looked around the space that had sheltered him for two months now. "I think to be safe, we need to leave."

"We can go to the Rangers," she said. "It's time we asked for their help."

He liked the way she said "we," as if he wasn't alone in this anymore. "There's another problem," he said. He took the flyer from his pocket, unfolded it and handed it to her.

She squatted and held the paper in the light of the lantern. Her expression contorted into one of dismay. "They think I'm dangerous?" Her voice rose, a hint of hysteria in the last word.

"Terrell must have sold them some story about the two of us attacking him and shooting out his windows," he said. "Remember, he has a habit of portraying me as the bad guy."

"I didn't think he saw me," she said.

"I don't think he did, but he knew from your voice that you were a woman. If investigators recovered any of the bullets, they might have linked them to the ammunition the Rangers use. And the Rangers were already searching for a missing woman, so I imagine they connected the dots and came up with you." He lowered himself to her level and squeezed her shoulder. "This doesn't mean they think you're a criminal.

They probably think I kidnapped you and forced you to do my bidding or something."

"Then they don't know me very well." The sadness in her eyes deepened. "But then, they really don't know me. I didn't make much of an effort to get close to them." She closed her eyes and sat back, arms wrapped around her knees. "What are we going to do?"

"We could still go to the Rangers," he said. "Tell them the whole story."

"I'm afraid," she said. "If they think I've gone rogue—if they believe Terrell instead of me—what chance do we have?" She stared at him. "For so long I thought you were exaggerating when you said it wasn't safe for you to trust law enforcement. All of a sudden, I know just how you feel."

"Except neither of us is alone now." He put his arm around her and pulled her close. "Whatever happens, we'll face it together." It was the kind of support he had taken for granted during his army career. Losing it had been one of the toughest adjustments to civilian life. He'd thought he was tough, that he actually preferred going it alone. Faith was showing him how wrong he had been, and how important it was to know that someone had your back, and that you could be there for them, too.

"FAITH MARTIN DEFINITELY drove the FJ." Beck approached the computer where Hud sat late Saturday, Carmen looking over his shoulder. "The fingerprints on the driver's door and dash are hers."

"What about the prints on the passenger side?" Carmen asked.

"The techs only got one good one," Beck said. "But it's a match for Trask."

"They drove the FJ to Terrell's neighborhood." Hud enlarged the map he had pulled up on his computer screen. "From the parking area where we found the vehicle, to this utility easement on the edge of Terrell's neighborhood. They parked right here, beneath the cell phone tower." He hit another key and an image of the landscape at the base of a cell tower sharpened into view.

"They must have hiked in to Terrell's place from there," Beck said. "But why?"

"Not to shout threats and shoot out his windows," Carmen said. "There would be no point in it."

"Terrell said Trask wanted to kill him," Beck said.

"Then why didn't he?" Carmen asked. "Terrell didn't have a scratch on him. Only one of the bodyguards was hurt, and he's going to make a full recovery. We didn't find any other blood at the scene, or anything to indicate that either Trask or Faith was injured." She leaned over the computer again. "Does that program show anywhere else Faith and Trask drove?"

Hud scrolled down the map, hit a series of keys then shook his head. "They took the FJ from our parking lot, to this parking space, then, the next night, from their parking spot to Terrell's neighborhood, and back." He leaned forward and squinted at the screen. "The timing of their trip to Terrell's matches up with his story."

"I wonder what he was getting rid of or cleaning up in the six hours it took him to notify us," Carmen said.

"Erasing his security tapes, for one," Beck said. "Rehearsing what he and the guards were going to say."

"I wish we could get a warrant to go into the house," Hud said. "Or to check out that guesthouse and Quonset hut in the backyard. I bet we'd find a different story if we could."

"We don't have any proof that Faith or Trask made it past the front yard," Carmen said. "And I'm betting Terrell knows a lot of lawyers, and probably a lot of judges, too. We're not going to get a warrant to go snooping just because the situation looks suspicious to us."

"Faith and Trask must have gone to Terrell's house because they wanted something from him," Hud said. "Maybe Faith shot out the windows to try to scare him into complying."

"All right," Carmen said. "But what did they want?"

"Something to do with TDC," Beck said. "From the very beginning, Trask has accused TDC of breaking the law. Those flash drives he left with his administrative assistant and later, with his former girlfriend, contained evidence that TDC was falsifying reports to the EPA."

"And we finally figured that out," Carmen said. "Also that TDC had donated land for a school, land that they knew was contaminated. And they dumped the contaminated material they removed while building the school onto public land. But TDC says all the blame lay with Mitch Ruffino—and we haven't been able to prove anything different."

"I've never believed Ruffino pulled all that off without Terrell, Davis, and Compton knowing about it," Hud said.

"After everything came out about the school, the FBI investigated TDC's finances and everything they found pointed back at Ruffino," Carmen said. "Terrell and the other partners came out squeaky clean."

"Maybe Trask knows they're not and went to confront Terrell," Hud said.

"If he did that, he's being stupid," Carmen said. "Then again, he hasn't made very many smart moves throughout this whole fiasco."

"So how did Faith get mixed up with him?" Beck asked. "She seemed pretty sharp to me. And the few times I heard her talk about Trask, she didn't seem to think much of him."

"When we find her, that's one of the first questions I'm going to ask," Carmen said.

"Meanwhile, I think we need to keep an eye on Terrell." Hud looked up at Carmen.

Beck nodded. "We really should," he said. "For his own protection."

"Trask and his mysterious female sidekick might decide to attack him again," Hud said. "If they do, we want to be there to catch them."

"And if Terrell is up to something suspicious, we want to be in position to find out what that something is." Carmen nodded. "We'll have to clear it with the commander."

"Then let's do it." Hud closed the computer program and rolled back his chair. "We can't get a warrant, but we don't have to have one to watch someone, especially if it's for their own protection."

"Terrell probably wouldn't agree," Carmen said.

Hud nodded. "That's why we're not going to ask him."

Chapter Sixteen

"We've got to go back to Terrell's place," Dane said. He and Faith lay together in his sleeping bag on Sunday morning, her head on his shoulder. She had been half dozing, and wasn't sure she had heard him right.

She snuggled more closely against him. "I don't want to go anywhere right now," she murmured.

He slid his arm from around her shoulders. "We need to get back to Terrell's as soon as possible."

Faith shifted so that she could look at him. "No more snooping around there," she said. "It almost got us killed."

"He knows that we know what's in that eighteen-wheeler," Dane said. "He destroyed my phone with the photographic evidence, but there's still my testimony to worry about."

"Which is why he wants you dead," she said.

"Maybe, but more than that, he'll be in a hurry to move everything off his property. I want to be there to see where he takes it."

"If he called the Rangers out to his house to tell

them about us, he's probably already moved everything," she said.

Dane shoved into a sitting position. She couldn't see him in the darkness, but she could feel him, his thighs even with her head now. "The trailer was in the Quonset hut, but I didn't see the tractor anywhere, did you?" Not waiting for her answer, he rushed on. "The trailer was almost full—there must have been thousands of bricks of heroin. It would have taken hours to unload it, and then, where were they going to put it? I think Terrell probably gambled that the Rangers wouldn't be able to snoop around his property without a warrant. But as soon as they left, he started planning where to shift his operation."

She sat upright, also. "Then we're probably already too late."

"I don't think so," he said. "For one thing, he'd have to move everything at night. For another, he can't stash a whole eighteen-wheeler full of drugs, not to mention whatever other part of the operation he's relocated to his home, in a matter of hours. He'd have to scout out a good place to stash the goods and make arrangements to protect the cargo. My guess is, he'll move everything tonight."

Faith felt alongside the sleeping bag until she found her headlamp. She switched it on then pulled it onto her head. "How are we going to get there?" she asked. "We don't have the FJ anymore, and it's miles away."

"We'll have to steal a vehicle." He said it as if he was suggesting they try a new trail route.

"Dane, no!" she said. "Auto theft is a felony. Besides, we're supposed to be relocating this evening. You said you knew a different cave we could hide in."

"You don't want to spend the rest of your life hiding with me," he said. "And you don't want to commit a felony—I understand that. Maybe you should go back to the Rangers. I'll continue on my own."

Her heart jerked in its rhythm. "You want me to leave?"

"I don't want you to go," he said. "But I've gotten you in enough trouble already. You should leave now, while it's still safe for you to do so."

"And you'll steal a car and go to Terrell's house by yourself."

He looked away, but his silence was answer enough.

"I can't let you face Terrell alone," she said. "Come with me to Ranger headquarters."

"Where they'll arrest me for kidnapping a law enforcement officer and who knows what other charges." He set his jaw in a hard line. "I'd rather take my chances with Terrell. At least I have a chance of stopping him."

"Like you stopped him last time? You could have been killed!"

"If I can't go alone and you won't come with me, what can I do?"

"Don't go!" She fisted her hands, fighting the urge to shake him.

He moved out of the sleeping bag and stood, his naked body sliding in and out of the beam of the headlamp a momentary distraction. "Get your things together and I'll walk partway up the trail with you."

Faith scrambled to her feet. "What am I supposed to tell the Rangers?"

"Tell them anything you want, though I'd appreciate it if you didn't tell them where you think I'm going."

"I could tell them about this place," she said.

"Go ahead. Because I won't come back here after I leave with you today."

She grabbed his arm as he moved past her. "I won't leave you," she said.

"If you were smart, you would."

"I'm smart enough to know you need me. Your lone wolf act hasn't been working for you, has it?"

He turned to face her, both of them naked, his chest almost brushing the tips of her breasts, his expression fierce in the glow of her headlamp. "What do you want me to say? That I'm not grateful for all you've done? That I don't care for you in a way I never thought I'd care for anyone again? That I don't love you? Because I can't say that—not even if doing so would drive you away. I'm good at a lot of things, but lying isn't one of them."

She drew him to her and kissed him with all the passion she was capable of, tears stinging her eyes then overflowing until they both tasted salt. When his arms reached around her, she pulled away. "If you're going to do this, you have to do it right," she said. "Don't charge over there without a plan."

"You're the planner, not me."

"It's about time you realized that." She turned away and grabbed up her pants. "Get dressed. We've got work to do."

Twenty minutes later, they were standing at the entrance to the cave, each with a loaded pack that contained all his gear, their clothes and the rest of their food. Sunlight illuminated the entrance, overly bright. "We're going to go out a different way," he said. "It'll be a tougher climb, but we're less likely to encounter other hikers. Or a Ranger Brigade officer with a tracking dog."

"How long do you think it will take us to get to TDC headquarters?"

"About four hours. It will take us two to get out of the canyon, then another two to hike to TDC. Unless you want to try borrowing a car from a tourist in the park."

"No." She hadn't wanted to steal a car at all, though he had finally persuaded her that "borrowing" a fleet car from TDC was a lesser evil.

"Then you'd better be prepared to walk."

After so many hours underground, the sunlight hurt her eyes, even behind the sunglasses Dane had loaned her. He had half a dozen pairs in the cave all found, he explained, while hiking around the park. "That and water bottles are the two most commonly lost items," he said. "I pick them up because I don't want them littering the park."

That was Dane—he didn't blink at stealing a car but wouldn't think of littering.

When he had said the climb would be rough, he

hadn't been exaggerating. For the next two hours, Faith dragged herself up steep inclines and rocky cliffs, breaking every fingernail and tearing a hole in one knee of her khaki uniform pants. By the time they reached the top, she was sweating and sore, and the thought of having to hike for two more hours with this pack on her back made her want to cry.

"You can still back out if you want," Dane said, handing her a water bottle. "I won't hold it against you."

"No." She drank deeply then capped the bottle and handed it back. "I'll be fine." She wasn't going to quit now. Dane was smart and tough and capable, but he couldn't do this alone. He'd proved that at Terrell's on Friday night.

They set out again, crossing rugged wilderness where few tourists ever ventured. A hot breeze dried her sweat. Dane stopped every fifteen minutes or so to check their bearings with a compass and topo map. After the first hour, Faith called a halt so she could affix duct tape over the blisters forming on both feet. Dane watched her work, saying nothing, for which she was grateful.

The headquarters of TDC Enterprises came into view before she realized what she was looking at. The seven-story office building, constructed of sandstone the same color as the surrounding rock, rose up from a sheltered hollow, its rounded corners blending with the weathered stone. "We're lucky it's Sunday," Dane said. "The building will be almost empty."

"You're sure you can steal a car?" she asked. "I've

arrested people for it before, but I have no idea how to do it."

"In this case, it doesn't take a genius," he said. "The fleet cars that aren't being used are parked in the back lot, unlocked, their keys under the front floor mat."

She gaped. "You're kidding."

He shrugged. "They're behind a fence, and there's on-site security. And no one has ever stolen one before, that I'm aware of. I guess that makes them complacent."

"So how are you going to get past the locked gate and the guard?"

"It's one guard. I'll wait until he's on the other side of the building. The lock on the gate isn't anything special. I'll cut it off." They had agreed that Faith would wait for him away from the building. Legally, she was still an accessory to the crime, but not actively participating assuaged her conscience.

He handed her the binoculars, straightened his clothes and ran a hand through his hair. "You'll need to carry both packs down to the highway," he said. "I'll pick you up there."

He strode off, taking an oblique path down to the building, keeping a large rock formation between him and the view from that side of the office building.

Faith knelt between the packs and raised the binoculars to follow him. He moved easily, not hurrying, but with long strides that closed the distance rapidly. His hair was too long and his clothing was worn and needed washing, but there was nothing furtive or downtrodden in his erect posture or the straight set of his shoulders. He was a man whose mood wasn't dependent on his situation, and that was one of the things that both enthralled and confounded her about him.

When he had vanished from sight around the side of the building, she stowed the binoculars and slipped his pack—the largest and heaviest of the two—onto her back and stood, staggering a little until the weight was balanced. Then she picked up the other pack and set out across the rough terrain, headed toward the stretch of pavement just visible on the horizon.

DANE STOOD IN a shadowed alcove at the corner of the building, cigarette butts on the pavement and the lingering stench of tobacco smoke attesting to the popularity of this retreat with the building's smokers. From here he had a good view of the back lot, and the row of three white sedans that served as fleet vehicles for the engineers and techs who occasionally needed to drive to a site to conduct testing. The vehicles bore no logo, merely a "fleet" indication on the license tag.

He pressed closer to the building, deeper into the shadows, as a truck drove past, the window rolled down, a man in a blue uniform shirt driving with one elbow resting on the sill. He kept his eyes on the lot, never glancing toward Dane's hiding place.

When the truck had disappeared around the corner of the building, Dane headed for the lot. He moved casually, head down, one hand in the pocket of his khaki hiking pants, jingling an imaginary set of keys.

If the guard happened to glance back, he'd see one of the techs taking a fleet vehicle for a Sunday afternoon inspection of an idle job site, or maybe an early-morning trip tomorrow to a location where he was to conduct testing. Nothing suspicious. Certainly nothing worth turning around for.

He moved to the end car. Less obvious it was missing, if the guard had bothered counting. Crouching beside it, he eased open the driver's-side door and felt under the mat. Yep—keys right there. Forcing himself to relax, he stood and slid into the seat and started the engine. The vehicle had a full tank of gas. That might prove useful.

He backed out of the slot and drove sedately toward the gate. The gate was locked. When someone checked out one of the fleet vehicles, they were issued a key to unfasten the lock. Dane left the car running and ambled to the gate, still doing his impression of an innocent tech.

Shielding the lock from the view of anyone passing by—and the security camera mounted on the fence to his right—he fastened the jaws of his multitool around the chain just behind the lock. It took some muscle, but the link finally snapped. Leaving the lock in place, Dane unwound the chain and opened the gate. He drove the car through, then got out and closed the gate and rewound the chain. From even a short distance, it looked as if the lock was still doing its job to keep everything behind it secure.

He drove slowly through the empty employee lot, and onto the private road that led to the highway. He slowed at the first big curve and Faith stepped onto the shoulder, her thumb in the air.

He stopped and she opened the back door, shoved both packs inside then hurried around to the passenger side. "Did you have any trouble?" she asked.

"No." He glanced at her. "It's going to be fine. You'll see."

"Nothing about this has been fine." She hesitated then put a hand on his arm. "Being with you has been wonderful, but the circumstances could have been better."

He nodded, though he wasn't sure he agreed. Under other circumstances, would he have been able to see what a remarkable woman she was? Would she have fought so hard both with him and for him? Would he have realized this was a woman he couldn't lead, but one he was willing to follow—even better, that Faith Martin was a woman he could walk beside? She wasn't as physically strong as he was, but that didn't matter because she was smarter and had a moral compass that guided her straight and true, while he too often fumbled around, figuratively lost if not mentally so.

He slowed the car at the turnoff for the utility easement for Terrell's development. The plan was to wait for full dark and then hike to Terrell's place. From there, they had several options to choose from, depending on what they found. "We're going to have to be really careful," she said as he parked the car and switched off the engine.

"You're always careful," he said. "And I'm learning how to be better at it."

She unfastened her seat belt, one hand on the door, but instead of getting out of the car, she turned to him. "Whatever happens tonight, I just want you to know I think I'm falling in love with you."

He smiled, even as his heart squeezed. "Always cautious, aren't you." He reached out to clasp her hand before she could protest. "I'm not complaining. We've already established that I'm the impulsive, reckless one." He kissed her. "I don't have to qualify," he said. "I do love you."

"You don't think whatever this is between us is intensified by danger and a sense of adventure? Two people in extreme circumstances who turn to each other?"

Her eyes searched his. As if he knew the answer to a question like that. "I don't know," he said. "But I think there's more to it than that. I'm hoping to stick around a while to find out."

Faith nodded and flashed the briefest of smiles. "Yeah. Me, too."

She got out of the car, but he sat for a moment longer, her question still running through his mind. What would it be like to live with a woman like this in a world where he wasn't struggling to survive? He hoped he got the chance to find out. The adrenaline rush of danger had a way of heightening emotion, but the mundane gave feelings a chance to deepen. The emotions Faith had kindled in him felt like seedlings with the potential to grow strong roots. Roots that could withstand the fiercest storm.

"I CAN'T BELIEVE I thought this was a good idea," Hud said as he scratched furiously at his ankle.

"You're the one who sat in the ant bed." Carmen raised the binoculars to her eyes and scanned the back of the Terrell property. She and Hud were crouched in the backyard of a vacant second home up the hill from Terrell's place. With the binoculars, they had an excellent view into the backyard. Jason Beck was stationed across the street in front of the house. The commander had agreed to this surveillance, but wouldn't spare more than the three of them, and they were limited to no more than six hours of overtime—unless something happened that required further investigation. So far, they'd been out there five hours and nothing had happened.

"Anything?" Hud asked, looking up from his scratching.

"Nothing. I know someone is in the guesthouse, because they walk by the window every once in a while, but nothing else is moving."

Hud checked his phone. "Beck says nothing is happening out front, either." He tucked the phone away. "I'd like to get a look at whatever is in that Quonset hut."

"You just want to see Terrell's collection of antique cars."

"That would be cool. If there really are cars in there. I did a little research online last night. I read about five profiles of Terrell in various publications and not one of them mentioned his hobby."

"He's the head of a multinational corporation. Maybe the profilers weren't interested in his hobbies," she said.

"The articles talked about his love of skiing and sailing. And one had a picture of him in his wine cellar. I don't think they'd leave out something like a big car collection."

"Maybe it's a new interest."

"Are you always so reasonable? How does Jake stand it?"

Carmen lowered the binoculars and smiled. "Jake would probably tell you I can be plenty unreasonable. But really, I just like to wind you up. I'd like to see inside that hut, too. But mainly because I'm nosy, not because I think there's anything illegal in there."

"I'm wondering if it's some huge indoor grow operation," Hud said. "And those three 'employees' aren't guards but gardeners."

"Growing marijuana isn't illegal in Colorado now."

"Growing a bunch of it without a permit is." He leaned around her and snatched up the binoculars.

"What are you doing?" she protested.

"I saw some movement." He peered through the glasses. "Someone is opening those big gates into the backyard."

Carmen rose onto her knees. Even from this distance, she could see the gates swing open and a big-rig tractor back into the yard, right up against the fence.

"Two men just came out of the guesthouse," Hud

said. "I think it's Pete and Ryan." His phone began vibrating. "Check my phone, will you? It's probably Beck."

She retrieved the phone and read the message from Beck. "'Eighteen-wheeler backing into the yard now. Terrell came out and talked to the driver, then went back inside.'"

"The two guys are opening up the Quonset hut." Hud swore. "There's a trailer in there. One of the big ones. It fills the whole hut. The tractor is hooking up to it."

"The trailer could be full of cars," she said, not really believing the words but needing to point this out.

"Why move them at night?" Hud asked, never looking away from the scene below.

Carmen tried to make out more in the dimness. Shadowy figures moved in and out of the hut and around the tractor-trailer combo. Then movement out of the corner of her eye distracted her. She nudged Hud's elbow. "Someone else is coming," she said. "Along the back fence. I think they're trying to stay out of sight."

Hud swiveled the binoculars to focus on the back fence line. The two figures kept to the deepest shadows, one moving up, then the other, drawing closer and closer to the activity in Terrell's backyard. Hud swore again then shoved the binoculars into Carmen's hand. "Take a look," he said. "Tell me what you think."

Carmen focused the binoculars. "It looks like a man and a kid. No—a woman. A short woman." A chill raced up her spine. Faith was short—the shortest officer on the force. "But what are they doing down there?"

"I think they're doing the same thing we are," Hud said. "They're spying on Terrell. And maybe for the same reason. Trask has always said TDC was up to no good. Maybe he was right."

FAITH PEERED OVER Dane's shoulder as he crouched against the palisade fence, staring at the confusion of lights and noise at the back of Terrell's property. The idling engine of the eighteen-wheeler vibrated through her, and the harsh clank of metal as the trailer was connected made her jump. "I told you they'd try to move the drugs out tonight," Dane whispered.

"Great. You were right. What do we do now?"

He dug in his pack and pulled out the cheap camera he had stopped and purchased at a convenience store on the way over, and began snapping off photographs. "You're not going to get much without a flash," she said.

"I'm taking a lot of shots," he said. "Maybe the Rangers have a tech wizard who can enhance them."

She closed her eyes and counted to ten. *Now* he was counting on the Rangers to get them out of a jam. If only her fellow officers didn't toss them both in jail the moment they laid eyes on them. Did she have enough savings to afford a decent lawyer? She'd have to rely on a public defender. The media would go wild over the story of a cop who went rogue after hooking up with the local outlaw. She'd never be able to show her face in town again—if she didn't end up in prison.

Dane nudged her. "Come on. I want to get closer."

"And do what?" But he either didn't hear her or pretended he hadn't.

A man—one of the guards they had dealt with yesterday—emerged from the front of the Quonset hut and walked up to the driver's cab. She could hear his raised voice over the idling engine, but couldn't make out the words. Meanwhile, a second guard came around the other side of the truck and walked up to the gate.

"Could you shoot out his tires?" Dane asked.

"No." As soon as she started shooting, all hell would break loose.

"No, because the tires are too tough?"

"No, because it's a terrible idea." The more distance she gained from their previous visit to Terrell's home, the more embarrassed she was about all the shooting she'd done. Yes, she'd done it to save Dane, but a little more subtlety might have been just as effective.

The first guard stepped back and the eighteen-wheeler's engine roared to life. "We need to stop him from leaving," Dane said, and started forward.

Faith grabbed him and pulled him back. "We don't need to do any such thing," she said. "We need to head back to the car and wait. When the truck turns onto the highway, we follow him to see where he goes."

"What if he goes all the way back to Mexico?"

"He won't take drugs back into Mexico," she said. "He'll want someplace close until he can offload the cargo. Those drugs are worth a fortune. He's not going to pass up the opportunity to sell them."

"You're right. We'd better hurry if we're going to meet the truck."

They turned and started down the fence line, the route familiar now, their steps surer, so they made almost no sound, almost invisible in the shadows.

"Stop right there. This is the police!"

Faith gasped and turned to see two shadowy figures to their right. She couldn't make out their features, but the voice had a ring of familiarity that made her heart sink. She winced and put up a hand to shield her eyes as the powerful beam of a light hit her in the face.

"Faith Martin and Dane Trask, we're taking you into custody," said the voice she knew belonged to one of her fellow Rangers.

Chapter Seventeen

Dane's first instinct was to fight. But all that would get him was Tasered, if not shot. He could feel Faith trembling beside him as the two officers—one man and one woman, in the khaki uniforms of the Ranger Brigade—moved toward them. "Carmen. Hud." Faith addressed the two officers. "I can explain."

"You don't need to arrest her," Dane interrupted. "She didn't do anything wrong. I kidnapped her and asked her to help me." He'd started to say "forced" her to help, but he could only imagine how indignant Faith would be at any attempt to portray her as a helpless victim.

"He needed help," Faith said. "And we can explain everything back at Ranger headquarters. But right now you need to know that a tractor-trailer rig is leaving Charles Terrell's home, with a fortune in heroin in its trailer."

The male officer, Hud—Dane recognized him as the man who had been with Audra the last few times he'd seen her—hesitated in the act of pulling flex-cuffs from his utility belt. "How do you know there's heroin in the trailer?" he asked.

"Because I got inside that Quonset hut Friday night and saw it," Dane said. "The trailer is almost full of what I'm sure are bricks of heroin. TDC has been bringing up drugs from Mexico and distributing them across three states for at least two years now. They were storing them in the tunnels at the Mary Lee Mine."

"Two years and you're just now getting around to telling us about it?" Carmen asked.

"It's a long story and I promise we'll explain later," Faith said. "Right now you need to seize those drugs."

Hud looked at Carmen then at Faith. "You're sure about this?"

"Yes." Even as she said the words, doubt made her queasy. She hadn't actually seen the drugs herself— she was merely taking Dane's word for it. What if it was all a lie?

"We're going to need backup," Carmen said. "And that's going to take time."

"The truck is leaving now," Dane said. "You need to follow it and find out where it's going."

Hud stepped forward, restraints in hand. "You'll come with us and we'll follow the truck."

Shame filled Faith as Carmen fastened the flex-cuffs on her wrist. She couldn't look at her fellow officer—if she even was a fellow officer. Maybe after all this, Faith would be thrown off the force.

"This way," Carmen said, taking Faith's arm and helping her up the slope behind the Terrell estate. The four of them walked in silence through a neighboring property, to the Ranger Brigade cruiser parked at the dark end of a cul-de-sac. Faith and Dane sat side by side in the backseat, hands bound and seat belts fastened. Faith wanted to ask to have her hands freed, but pride kept her silent.

Hud started the engine and headed out of the neighborhood. Carmen typed on her phone. "I'm letting Beck know to meet us at the highway," she said then turned in her seat to look at Faith. "You'll need to give an official statement later, but right now I want to know what happened at Terrell's place yesterday morning."

"We knew he had moved the drugs from the Mary Lee Mine," Faith said. "So we tried to think where he might have relocated the operation. Dane knew he had this place—big, remote and secure. We decided to check it out to see if we saw anything suspicious."

"You stole the spare FJ to get here," Hud said.

She winced. "I'm still a Ranger. And I was investigating a crime." The defense sounded weak, even to her ears, but she forced herself to hold her head up and meet his gaze. She was already in big trouble. Speaking up for herself wasn't going to make it any worse.

Carmen shifted her attention to Dane. "You went inside the Quonset hut?"

"I cut a hole in the side first, to look inside," he said. "I saw the trailer, so I unzipped the back and went in. The trailer was open and I could see the drugs inside."

"So how did Faith end up shooting out Terrell's

front windows and wounding his employee?" Hud asked.

"Two of Terrell's bodyguards caught Dane in the trailer, beat him up and hauled him into the house," Faith said. "I knew they'd kill him if I didn't stop them. I didn't have a phone or any way of calling for help, so I planned to go back to the vehicle and drive to Ranger headquarters and call from there. But before I could leave, I saw them, with Terrell and a third man, come out of the house. They were moving Dane to a vehicle. I knew I didn't have time to go for help, so I shot out the tire on the SUV to keep them from leaving. Then I shot out the windows to frighten Terrell into letting Dane go."

"And the guard?" Carmen asked.

"He rushed at me, so I disabled him." She swallowed. She had no idea what Terrell had told them, but she needed to stick to the truth. "Then I kept my gun aimed at Terrell and threatened to kill him if he didn't let Dane go. So he ordered his men to release him."

"They just let you walk away?" Hud asked.

"They came after us, but they weren't very organized and we managed to evade them," Dane told them.

"We found the FJ where you'd parked it," Hud said.

"I know," Dane said.

"So where have you been hiding out all this time?" Hud asked.

Dane didn't answer.

"How did you get back here tonight?" Carmen asked.

"I borrowed one of TDC's fleet cars," Dane said. "They keep the keys in them."

"You stole one of their cars," Hud said.

Dane set his jaw and said nothing.

They reached the intersection with the highway. "If you turn left and go about a hundred yards, you'll come to a utility easement," Faith said. "If you pull in there, you can watch for the tractor-trailer from cover."

Hud did as she instructed, and parked the cruiser beneath a clump of trees well off the highway. He turned to Faith. "Did he really kidnap you?"

She bit her lip.

"I did," Dane said. "I was desperate to get someone to listen to me and figured she would be someone who could help."

"You know, Ranger headquarters is open all day, seven days a week," Hud said. "And there's this great device called a telephone that you can use to get in touch with us."

"Terrell was trying to kill him," Faith said. "He didn't know who he could trust. Terrell also threatened his daughter if Dane talked to anyone."

Hud's expression darkened at the mention of his girlfriend, Audra Trask. "I can protect Audra," he said.

"You can't be with her twenty-four hours a day," Dane noted. "I'm not sure you realize how much money and how many people Terrell has at his disposal. People who don't even blink if they're paid to murder someone. They did it to that reporter, and to the man in the Jeep at the BLM camping area. They made it look like an overdose, but it wasn't."

"Larry Keplar told me he had found some files at TDC that he thought showed evidence of criminal activity," Faith said. "He thought they were evidence of Dane's guilt, but TDC must have worried that if he turned those files over to law enforcement, we'd figure out what was really going on. So they killed Larry."

"And they probably destroyed the files," Dane said. "That's been a big problem all along. Every time I found evidence, they destroyed it. So I decided to try to focus law enforcement attention on their other crimes. I hoped someone would visit the Mary Lee Mine to investigate and find the heroin I saw there, or look into the company's trucking operation and notice all the cargo coming from Mexico and question it. I thought if I didn't talk directly about the drug operation, I could protect Audra."

Hud opened his mouth to respond, but Carmen said, "There's the truck."

The eighteen-wheeler turned onto the highway and slowly rolled past them. The driver's door of the tractor bore the legend Ace Trucking. The silver trailer was unmarked. When the truck was well past, Hud shifted into gear and pulled forward. He kept well back, the red lights on the rear of the trailer easy to follow in the darkness.

"What did Terrell tell you about our visit the other night?" Dane asked. "We saw the Wanted poster with Faith's and my pictures, so I assume he called you."

"He said you and some wild woman he couldn't identify showed up and started shooting up the place," Hud said.

"Did you believe him?" Faith asked.

Hud glanced in the rearview mirror. "It seemed pretty out of character for you, but then, so does hiding out with a wanted man."

Dane didn't do anything wrong, and neither did I, she thought, but said nothing.

The radio chirped and Carmen answered it. "Do we want to pull this guy over?" Beck asked. "We could say we need to check his paperwork."

"We're just going to see where he's going," Hud said. "We don't want trouble."

They followed the truck until it turned off at a closed gas station. Hud slowed then stopped on the shoulder. Beck pulled his cruiser in behind them. "They'll spot us if we try to follow on that narrow road," Hud said.

"I don't think there's an outlet," Beck said. "I'm pretty sure that road dead-ends at the lake, I think at a boat storage yard."

"Then he's probably going to park there, maybe move the drugs into storage," Hud concluded.

"The bricks of heroin are inside plastic barrels labeled as FertiRain," Dane said. "It's a fertilizer they spray on corn."

"Load a few barrels on a helicopter or a spray plane and nobody thinks anything of it," Beck said. "You could transport it almost anywhere."

"We need to get these two back to headquarters." Hud indicated Faith and Dane.

"I'll stay here and keep an eye out for the trailer," Beck said.

"We'll contact the sheriff and DEA for backup," Carmen said. "We need to move quickly."

"What about them?" Beck nodded to Faith and Dane.

What about us? Faith silently echoed.

"I think the commander is going to be very interested in what they have to say," Hud said.

Will he believe us? Faith wondered. *And is my career—and maybe life as I know it—over?*

COMMANDER GRANT SANDERLIN reminded Dane of every general he'd ever met—clean-cut, upright and no-nonsense. He didn't try to hide his annoyance with them, but he showed his displeasure with excessive correctness. He introduced himself, explained in clipped tones their rights and the process for taking their statements. He addressed all his comments to Dane, not even looking at Faith.

Faith felt the snub, Dane was sure. She was quiet, cowed even, the defiant spirit that had drawn him to her buried under a posture of shame. He wanted to tell her she had done nothing wrong. Everything bad was his fault. Did she think he had ruined her life? Was the connection he felt with her already withering away, something that could only survive in seclusion?

Officer Hudson had left to deal with coordinating a raid on the tractor-trailer and Terrell's estate. Officer

Redhorse had stayed to take Faith's and Dane's statements. "You can remove their restraints," the commander said, and Officer Redhorse cut them loose. "Though they'll be back in place if you give us any trouble," he added.

Faith rubbed her wrists and looked close to tears. Dane fought down his anger. She was one of them. They shouldn't be treating her like this.

"Deputy Martin, let's start with you," Sanderlin said, looking at Faith for the first time since he had entered the room. "Tell us what happened, starting with your last evening on duty."

Faith straightened a little, her hands flat on the table in front of her, her voice even, chin up, as if she was delivering unpleasant news to a superior. Her courage cheered him a little.

"I left work that evening and walked out to my car," she began. "Dane Trask accosted me, disarmed me, tied my hands and feet, and carried me off to his hideout."

"How did you feel about that?" Redhorse asked.

It was an odd question for an interrogation, but Faith didn't hesitate. "I was furious."

"She was," Dane said. "She put up quite a fight."

"We'll hear from you later," the commander said with a look that silenced him. "Go on, Deputy."

"After a while, he persuaded me that if I tried to run away, I'd likely kill myself stumbling around in the dark," Faith said. "He promised that if I would hear him out, he'd escort me back to the station in the morning."

"And what did he tell you?"

Faith summarized Dane's story, making light of what he now saw as some of his less wise choices, leaning a little heavier than he thought necessary on his fear for his life and the life of his daughter. All in all, he thought she made him look more hapless than heroic.

"After hearing all this, why didn't you return to Ranger Brigade headquarters the next day?" the commander asked.

She glanced at him, though he couldn't interpret the look. "I believed Dane when he said TDC had committed crimes," she said. "I believed they would commit more crimes if they weren't stopped. But I also knew that stopping them required proof. My hearsay testimony about what he had said wasn't going to be enough to get a warrant. Confronting TDC about our suspicions wasn't going to get the Ranger Brigade any further than it had gotten Dane, and it would alert TDC of our suspicions and give them time to either move or temporarily suspend their operation. So I decided I would try to gather as much evidence as I could—with Dane's assistance—before we brought it all to the Rangers."

Commander Sanderlin didn't look pleased. "If you had come to us, we could have organized an undercover investigation, or passed this on to the DEA to handle," he said. "Instead, you went outside of your authorized duties to investigate on your own, which resulted in you destroying private property, wounding a civilian and being an accessory to multiple vehicle thefts. All while leaving your colleagues and other law enforcement officers to devote valuable time searching for you that could have been better spent on other investigations."

"Yes, sir." Her cheeks flamed but her voice remained steady.

"We will defer the decision about whether or not to press criminal charges," Sanderlin said. "But you are suspended from your duties, pending further investigation."

"Yes, sir."

Dane wanted to take her hand, to reassure her he still supported her, if no one else did. But all he could do was sit in silence, angry on her behalf.

The commander turned to him. "Mr. Trask, your behavior has also eaten up valuable hours of law enforcement time, and possibly endangered others. Roy Holliday, in particular, might be alive today if he had not been researching an article about you, and therefore attracting TDC's displeasure."

"That's regrettable," Dane said. "But I didn't feel I had any choice in the matter." The commander was never going to see things his way, he knew. Maybe most people wouldn't. But he couldn't go back and change the past. "What matters now is stopping TDC," he continued. "I'm here now and I'll do what I can to help."

"You may be asked to testify at some later date," the commander said. "But for now, we do not need or desire your assistance."

"Are you charging me with a crime?" Dane asked.

"We're charging you with two counts of motor vehicle theft," Sanderlin said. "The Park Service may press further charges, related to your sending your pickup truck plummeting into Black Canyon, where it had to be retrieved at not inconsiderable expense."

"Will you be keeping him in custody?" Faith asked.

Sanderlin looked from her to Dane. "I'm willing to release you if you promise not to disappear again," he said.

"I promise." Dane said the words because he needed to, to stay free. But he wasn't sure he could keep that promise. If TDC came after him—as he was sure they would, once they discovered he had resurfaced in public—he would do what he had to do to save his life.

"That's all for now." The commander rose, the signal that they were dismissed.

"I can drive you to your home," Officer Redhorse said to Faith after the commander was gone.

"Dane needs to come with me," Faith said.

Carmen's gaze flickered to Dane. "It would look better for you if you kept your distance from him for a while," she said. "I'm not saying you'll be reinstated, but it might help."

"Dane is coming with me," Faith said, her face set in a stubborn expression he well recognized.

"All right," Carmen said. "Is there anything you need from your locker or desk? We have your purse and your phone."

"Thank you," Faith said. "I would like those."

"I'll get them and be right back. You can wait here."

As soon as they were alone, Dane turned to Faith. "You should take her advice," he said. "Associating with me isn't doing your reputation any favors."

"I've already lost my reputation," she said. "I don't want to lose you, too." She put her hand on his arm, commanding his attention. "TDC is going to come after you. We both know it. You'll be safer with me than you will be alone."

"I survived alone before."

"By running. You can't do that anymore."

He started to protest that he could, but the look in his eyes sent a different message: he couldn't keep running. He had to stand and fight. And she was ready to stand with him. "All right," he said. "We'll face this together."

"I'm counting on it," she said then turned away. But not before he caught the spark in her eyes that told him she hadn't yet given up on him. She hadn't given up on *them*.

Chapter Eighteen

Faith had only been away from home five days, but already her house had a stale, unlived-in atmosphere. Dane followed her inside, taking in the small but neat front room and even smaller, slightly messier, kitchen. "Shower first," she said. "Then food."

He followed her to the bedroom, but she shut the door in his face. Okay. Obviously she needed time alone to process this.

She hadn't said a word to him on the drive from Ranger Brigade headquarters. He'd put that down to the presence of Officer Redhorse, but her continued silence troubled him. As the shower beat a tattoo in the bathroom, he wandered through the living room and kitchen, a detective looking for clues about her private life.

The house was small, the rent probably on the cheaper side for the area, fitting in with her income as a law enforcement officer. But the place was clean, the walls painted bright white, red-and-blue cushions on the gray cloth sofa adding pops of color. She had a lot of books—mostly novels, and some decent art, including signed paintings from a couple of local artists he recognized.

Somehow, he had expected more cop stuff. Guns maybe. Or law enforcement books or magazines. If she had any of that, it was stowed away somewhere else.

The water shut off and Faith emerged from the shower. "There're towels in the cabinet," she said as she passed him in the hall a few minutes later.

He carried his backpack into the bathroom, and allowed himself to zone out to the bliss of a hot shower after so many weeks of cold river baths. He changed into his last set of semi-clean clothes and made a mental note to do a load of laundry as soon as possible. All these mundane thoughts crowded up against the underlying tension over the future.

He and Faith weren't under arrest—yet. The Rangers had made it clear they needed to stay put and not talk to anyone. That included his daughter, Audra. He wanted to talk to her, to let her know he was all right, but that would have to wait.

Clean and dressed, he returned to the kitchen, where Faith, dressed in shorts and a T-shirt, her hair still damp, stood at the stove. "I made bacon and eggs," she said. "You can butter the toast." She nodded toward the toaster.

Silently, they prepared breakfast and then sat across from each other at her small, two-person table to eat. She had made coffee, too, and he laced his liberally with the creamer she took from the refrigerator, and tried not to groan with pleasure as he ate. It was the best meal he had had in weeks. He said as much, but Faith only nodded and kept her head down.

When the last bite was eaten and almost the last drop of coffee drunk, he pushed aside his plate. "If you're not going to talk to me, this isn't going to work," he said.

One side of her mouth quirked up, as if she was holding back a smile. "I think that's supposed to be my line, isn't it? The woman whose partner won't tell her what he's feeling?"

"You don't have to gush or anything, but I'd like to know your plan for what's next." He leaned across the table toward her. "Because I know you have a plan."

She put her chin in her hand and looked out across the room. "I should probably call a lawyer."

"You're not charged with anything."

"No, but I probably will be."

"I'm sorry about the car theft," he said. "I shouldn't have let you anywhere near that. And don't worry about the lawyer. I'll pay for one."

"You *should* pay for one." But her smile was complete—if a little sad—this time. "I can't control what the Rangers do to me," she said. "But I am worried about Terrell. You know him better than I do. What do you think he'll do?"

"He may not know we're back among the living yet," Dane said. "It depends on how long it takes the press to find out."

"The Rangers were pretty good about not leaking things to the media," she said. "At least, when I was the public information officer, they were."

"You don't think they have someone on TDC's payroll?"

Her eyes widened. "No!"

"I'm not making idle accusations. I'm almost certain TDC was paying off someone with the sheriff's department—maybe even with the DEA. I think it's one reason they were able to operate on such a large scale for so long."

"No one on the Ranger Brigade is accepting bribes," she said. "I'm certain of it."

"That's good, then. They're going to seize that truck, and I thought I overheard something about a raid on Terrell's property. Once they find the heroin in the truck, they should be able to get a warrant to search the property, and probably TDC headquarters, too."

"Will they find anything?"

"There must be records somewhere," Dane said. "Communications with the trucking company and their suppliers in Mexico. Evidence of money laundering. It may take a while to dig out, but the DEA and the FBI have people who can do that."

"Terrell has lawyers who can keep him out of jail while they dig," she said. She stood and went to refill her coffee. "Now that I've been officially relieved of my duties, I have no idea what's going on. I won't know about any raid they make or charges they file against Terrell until I read about it in the paper."

"I'm sorry about that, too," he said. "I know your career was important to you."

Faith sipped her coffee, her brow furrowed. "I

liked it because I thought the work was important. I was doing something that mattered. And I liked being part of a tight-knit group. Law enforcement officers are an in-group that bond over experiences that no one else understands. They look after each other. I never had that before. I'm going to miss it."

"I get that," he said. "The military is like that, too."

"Do you miss it?" she asked. "Being a soldier?"

"I miss some of it. Not most of it. I never thought I could make a career of it." He stood and joined her in front of the coffee machine. "You can fight to get your job back," he said. "I'll swear I influenced you. You were in a vulnerable position and I took advantage of that."

She gripped her coffee mug with both hands. "I'm a competent adult. I made my own decision and, in spite of everything, I'm not sorry. If you don't understand that about me, you haven't been paying attention."

"I understand." He pulled her into his arms. "It's one of the things I love about you. I'm just afraid I've ruined your life and that's going to come between us."

She made a scoffing noise. "You haven't ruined my life."

"Talk to a lawyer," he said. "There must be some who specialize in defending law enforcement officers. You can get your job back."

She shook her head. "I don't deserve to have my job back."

He frowned. "What do you mean? You didn't do anything wrong."

"I did." She pulled back enough to look up at him. "I knew I should have gone back to the Rangers and let them handle the investigation. But I wanted to be the hero—to solve the problem myself. In doing so, I potentially screwed up the whole investigation. I could have been killed and so could you."

"You see all that now, but how could you have seen it then?"

"I did see it," she said. "And I decided to strike out on my own anyway." Her expression had softened when she met his gaze again. "I'm a lot like you in that regard. I liked being part of the team in my work, but I wasn't very good at it. I always held myself apart. I didn't have close friendships on the job, not like the other officers, especially the other women."

He caressed her shoulder. "That doesn't make you wrong," he said.

"I know that now. You helped me see that. It's okay not to fit in with the group. Some of us are like that. You're like that."

"I am," he said. He had fit in with the military. He had done a good job and remained loyal to his fellow soldiers. But he hadn't loved it enough to choose it as a career. He excelled as an engineer and had built up Welcome Home Warriors into a veterans organization he could be proud of. But he was always happiest on his own—alone in the wilderness.

Then he'd met Faith, and realized he had room in his life for one more. "What will you do now, if you can't be a law enforcement officer?" he asked.

"I don't know. But I'll find something." She pushed

him away. "In the meantime, you're right. We do need a plan. How are we going to deal with Terrell? Because I don't believe for a minute he's going to go away."

CARMEN STOOD WITH Hud and the commander and watched as DEA agents removed barrel after barrel filled with bricks of heroin from the eighteen-wheeler's trailer at the storage facility by the lake. An early morning raid had yielded the drugs and the arrest of three guards who hadn't put up much of a fight. The youngest of them was already asking for witness protection in exchange for his testimony.

"If Trask had come to us when he'd first learned of TDC's activities, who knows how many drugs we could have kept off the market?" Sanderlin said as an agent rolled yet another barrel past them.

"He said he didn't have any proof," Carmen said. "Would he have been able to persuade us to pursue the matter?"

"He was a veteran and an engineer with a good reputation," Sanderlin stated. "Of course we would have believed him."

Carmen wondered about that. TDC had a good reputation, too. They were one of the largest employers in the area, known for donating money to every worthy cause—and many an elected official's campaigns. Would Trask's accusations have counted for much against the weight of that kind of power?

"Trask and Audra might have very well been killed

for their trouble," Hud said. "Drug lords have murdered people for a lot less."

Sanderlin said nothing. Was his silence agreement? His phone rang and he answered it and turned away to talk. Hud moved closer to Carmen. "How did it go with Faith?" he asked.

"She's suspended," Carmen said. "I could tell she wasn't happy about it, but she was stoic."

"She couldn't have been surprised," Hud said. "She must have broken half a dozen regulations, not to mention the law."

Carmen nodded. "I checked, and she never had a single mark against her before this. Nothing but commendations."

"There's something between her and Trask," Hud said. "You saw it, didn't you?"

Carmen nodded. "She asked me to give him a ride to her place, too. I even told her keeping her distance from him might help her reputation, but she wouldn't hear of it."

"Love can make people do strange things."

Carmen thought of her own contentious courtship with the man who was now her husband. She had actually tried to arrest Jake when they'd first met, not knowing he was working undercover. They had clashed more than once over behavior she saw as reckless, yet in the end, she would have followed him anywhere.

Had it been like that for Faith? Had she believed staying with Dane Trask was the only way to save him? Did she still think he had been worth possibly losing her career?

The commander joined them again. "The sheriff's department seized a number of firearms and computer equipment and other material from Charles Terrell's home in Sunset Estates, and they arrested three men, but they say Terrell packed up and left this morning. So far, no one has been able to reach him."

"Maybe he got wind of what was up and left the country," Hud said.

"The sheriff doesn't think so. They found Terrell's passport in his home."

"He could have another passport under a different name," Carmen said.

"They're looking into that. Meanwhile, the DEA is handling things here."

"I need to check in with their commander," Hud, a DEA officer himself, said.

"Redhorse and I will go back to headquarters."

The commander waited until they were in his cruiser before he spoke. "What did you think of Faith's statement?" he asked.

She considered a moment before answering. "I think she acted rashly, but with good intentions."

"You think I was too hard on her."

"No, sir. I don't think you had any choice but to suspend her. I believe Faith knows that, too."

"I want to bring Trask in for questioning again," he said. "I'll send you and Beck to pick him up."

"Yes, sir."

"We need to find out more about Terrell's operation," Sanderlin said. "Trask has been following the man for months. If anyone has a sense of what Terrell's next move might be, I think it's Trask."

FAITH FOUND A notebook and pen and sat across from Dane at the table. "Planning time," he said, looking amused.

"I thought engineers were supposed to be very methodical," she said.

"I'm not that kind of engineer," he said. "I'm good with numbers, but I believe there's such a thing as overplanning."

"Not in this case," she said. "We have to think of everything if we're to be prepared for Terrell to come after us."

"Best-case scenario, the Rangers surprise him at home and bring him in for questioning," Dane said. "That buys us time."

"Then we'd better use that time wisely." She wrote "Supplies" at the top of the page and underlined it. "What do we need?"

He looked around the kitchen with its yellow-and-white curtains, and dirty breakfast dishes in the sink. "Are you planning to hold out here? We could use more firepower. I assume the Rangers relieved you of your duty weapon? They took my gun and my knife from my backpack—I assume while we were being questioned. There's a receipt, so it was all by the book."

"I have a 9 millimeter pistol and a small revolver."

"That's not going to get us very far."

"I don't want to shoot it out with Terrill," she said. "Mostly, I want to avoid him."

"So we're back to running."

She shook her head. "No. We need a better offense. I'm thinking we contact the press."

"You have to be careful there," Dane said. "You start accusing people of things, you can be sued for libel. And TDC still has a lot of influence in this area. One suspended cop and the local equivalent of Sasquatch aren't going to be a match for him and the media."

"I don't want to make this about us," she said. "I'm thinking we leak information about the raid on his home and the seizure of drugs in a tractor-trailer that was spotted leaving his house."

"You'll need to confirm the Rangers were successful before you leak that information," he said.

She chewed on the end of her pen. "I think Carmen might tell me," she said. She brightened. "Or you could call Audra, and she could ask Hud."

"I should call her," Dane said, pained at the thought of his daughter. They had always been close and he had missed her. "I've stayed away so long because I feared drawing more of TDC's attention to her."

"Let me try with Carmen first, then you can call Audra. She at least needs to know you're okay. And she needs to hear it from you, not Hud."

She crossed out "Supplies" and wrote "1. Call Carmen" and "2. Call Audra" on her list. "What else?"

"It would help if you could get your personal vehicle back from the Rangers," he said. "I don't like not being able to leave here in a hurry if we need to."

She added "3. Car" to her list and "4. Call newspapers?"

"I wonder if…"

But before she could finish the sentence, he held up a hand. "Shh."

She carefully laid down the pen and slowly turned to look toward the front of the house.

The vehicle moved slowly past the house, the engine a low hum in the stillness. When they could no longer hear it, Faith relaxed and picked up the pen again. "Do you know anyone at a newspaper or television station we could talk to?" she asked.

But Dane barely heard the question. A knot of tension tugged at his stomach. Carefully, avoiding making a sound, he stood and moved to the front window. Standing to one side, he peered around the edge of the drawn blinds. The street in front of her house was silent and empty.

"What is it?" she whispered. "You're freaking me out."

"Just a feeling." He shook his head and turned away from the window.

A flash of light, a shockwave of sound and the back door exploded open. Dane hurtled across the room, dragged Faith from her chair and shoved her to the ground, his body shielding her. He automatically groped at his side for a weapon, but of course, none was there.

Charles Terrell stepped through the shattered doorway, cradling a semiautomatic rifle. "Get up!" he ordered. "When I kill you I want you on your feet."

Chapter Nineteen

"If Trask balks about coming with us, we'll lean on Faith to talk some sense into him," Beck said as Carmen drove toward Faith's home for the second time that day.

"If you stress that we want his help, it might go over better," Carmen said. "Let him know his tip about the tractor-trailer was a good one."

"Right, 'we believe you now and though we still don't trust you, we're willing to give you the benefit of the doubt.'"

"Maybe not quite that honest, but yes."

"It feels weird, Faith being suspended," Beck said. "I always liked her."

"I still like her," Carmen said. "She just made some bad choices."

"Hud filled me in a little on her story. Bad move deciding to investigate on her own, but I get it. I might have felt the same, especially since she was trying to get away from working behind the desk all the time. She was trying to prove she was as good an investigator as any of us."

"And going about it the wrong way."

"Yeah. But I sympathize."

"Focus on Trask right now. And hope he really can help us find Terrell."

"Maybe a former fugitive can help us find a current one," Beck said.

They pulled up to the house, which looked deserted, the shades drawn and the driveway empty. "We need to see about getting Faith's car back to her," Carmen said.

They approached the front door and Beck rang the bell. It sounded in the house, an electronic chime. No answer.

"They don't have a car," Beck said. "They couldn't have left. Unless they called an Uber or something." He rang the bell again.

Carmen put up a hand to silence him and drew her weapon. She met his gaze and his expression hardened and he drew his own weapon. She indicated that she was moving to the back of the house. He nodded and took up a position to the left of the front door.

Carmen crept around the house, remaining out of sight of windows. She couldn't say what made her so sure something was wrong inside, but every sense had sharpened with awareness. As she passed along the side of the house, she thought she heard a muffled scraping, like something dragged along a rug. Then all went unnaturally still again.

At the back corner of the house, she paused, then, weapon raised, she peered cautiously around the corner. Her gaze first landed on a splintered chunk of wood that lay on the edge of the patio. From there, her gaze shifted to the back door—or what had been a back door, now merely pieces of broken wood framing an opening.

Still focused on the door, Carmen eased back, into the yard of the house next door, far enough away she thought she wouldn't be heard. She keyed her radio and spoke softly. "Ten thirty-eight. One four three five South Willow," she said. "And a possible ten thirty-one." Those were the codes for officer down and a possible hostage situation. Faith might be suspended, but she was still one of them, and that call would bring every officer in the vicinity descending on this house. She only hoped they weren't too late.

TERRELL'S COMMAND SENT an icy chill over Faith as she lay beneath Dane, his weight crushing her. "Get up!" Terrell barked again. "Now!"

Dane eased off her and stood, hands in the air. Faith did so, also, standing a little apart from Dane, making it harder for Terrell to kill them both with one shot. Though with that semiautomatic, it would only take a fraction of a second to mow them both down.

"The Rangers will be here any minute with my car," she said. "You should leave while you still can."

"I'm not leaving until I've shut him up for good." Terrell pointed the muzzle of the rifle at Dane. "You made a bad choice when you decided to team up with him."

Keep him talking, she thought. It was her only chance. He hadn't fallen for her bluff about the Rangers, but every second she kept him from pulling the trigger was one more second she had to come up with a plan to get them out of this.

She had to choke back hysterical laughter at the thought. What did she mean, get them out of this? Optimism was one thing, but she was obviously delirious if she thought two unarmed people were going to escape a madman with a powerful weapon, standing three feet away from them.

"I just want to know one thing before I die," Dane said. "One thing I could never figure out."

He had caught Terrell's interest. "What's that?"

"I knew what you were doing, bringing in drugs and selling them, but I was never able to find solid proof. I looked everywhere, too—you know I did. How did you hide the money, the contacts, everything that goes into a business that size—even an illegitimate one?"

"Because I approached it like a business," he said. "And I was smart. Some of it is out in the open, disguised as regular activities. It looks legit to law enforcement and to the IRS, but if anyone bothered to dig, they'd find out that school in rural Mexico or that office building in Afghanistan was never really built. Oh, there's a construction site there, maybe a shell, but all those orders for materials and payments for real estate were really for our other products."

"Do your partners know what you're doing?" Faith asked. "Davis and Compton."

"They know some of it," he said. "Enough not to

ask too many questions." He raised the rifle. "Enough talking. Time to say goodbye."

"Charles Terrell! The house is surrounded. Come out with your hands up!"

The blaring voice made Faith jump. Terrell turned his head, but kept the rifle trained on them, his finger hovering over the trigger. Faith looked around for somewhere—anywhere—to run. Dane moved closer to her, his hand grasping hers, keeping her from running. He nodded toward Terrell.

She followed his gaze, at first seeing only the man with the gun who wanted them dead. He looked back at them, the first hint of agitation in his eyes. "You weren't lying about the Rangers," he said.

"Of course not," she managed to admit. She had no idea what the Rangers were doing out there—or whoever had come to their aid, but she wasn't going to question it, even if she didn't normally believe in miracles. And right now, Terrell was standing near an open door, almost in sight, surely, of a law enforcement sniper. That sniper was their best chance to get out of there alive.

"You're going to get me out of here." Terrell grabbed her hand and dragged her to him, the rifle pressed across her chest, the end of the barrel digging into her neck. "If you try to come in here, I'll kill this officer!" he shouted.

For a dizzying moment, Faith flashed back to another man with a gun who had wanted to kill her. Another man trying to bargain with the police. She had gotten out of that situation—could she do it again?

Terrell squeezed her more tightly against him. Didn't he realize if he pulled the trigger he'd probably kill himself, as well? Maybe that didn't matter to him at this point.

But something else he didn't realize was that he had turned his back on Dane. She saw Dane take a step sideways, toward the kitchen counter and the rack of knives by the stove.

"You need to stand where they can see you," she told Terrell. "Where they can see that you have me."

He didn't question why she was being so helpful, merely shuffled sideways, dragging her with him, until they stood in the opening that had once been her back door.

"I've got her, and I'm going to kill her if you don't let me walk out of here," he shouted. The rifle barrel dug painfully into her throat, and she made a strangled sound. She wondered if she could kick his shin hard enough to make him let her go. But she was barefoot and in the struggle his finger might slip on the trigger.

He let out a strangled cry and loosened his hold enough for her to dive to the floor, moving to the side, scrabbling on her hands and knees for cover. Any kind of cover.

Then the sound of gunfire, but not from Terrell. He staggered backward, dropped his weapon, then sank to his knees, blood pouring from the wound in his chest from the law enforcement sniper.

Dane knelt beside her and pulled her into his arms.

"It's okay," he murmured, rocking her back and forth, his face buried in her hair. "It's okay. It's okay."

An officer in full SWAT gear appeared in the doorway. He raised his face shield and Lieutenant Michael Dance stared down at her. "Are you okay?" he asked.

Faith nodded then found her voice. "I'm okay."

"I'm okay." Dane raked a hand through his hair. "I feel about ten years older than I did this morning, but I'm okay."

Dance turned to Terrell and frowned. "Is that a knife in his back?" he asked.

"I knew I couldn't get close to him without risking him hurting Faith," Dane said. "But when he turned away, I grabbed a kitchen knife from the block by the stove and threw it."

Faith and Dance stared at him. "Is that something they teach you in the army?" she asked.

"Boy Scouts," Dane said. "Well, they didn't actually teach it, but you get a bunch of boys with pocketknives on a campout, they're going to practice throwing knives at trees. I was pretty good at it, so I kept it up."

"Uh-huh." Dance held out a hand to Faith. "Come on. We need to get you out of here while we process the scene. You, too," he said to Dane.

Outside, they sat together in a Ranger cruiser while officers streamed in and out of the house. The medical examiner, an ambulance and a forensics crew all had their turn. Dane kept his arm tight around Faith and neither of them spoke for a long time.

"Do you wish you were out there with them, working?" he asked after a while.

"You'd think I would be," she said. "But I'm not." She sighed. "This is too much like last year, when that father took me hostage."

"When you went in to save that little boy," he said.

"I saved the boy, but I did it wrong. Just like this time, with you." She laced her fingers with his. "I think to be a good cop, you have to follow the rules. Adhere to procedure. They're put into place to protect you and everyone else. I'm just not very good at doing that. I hate it's taken me this long to figure that out."

He raised her hand to his lips and kissed it. "I thought I knew all the answers, and then you came along and showed me I didn't," he said. "I never thought I could be grateful for something like that, but I am."

Faith smiled up at him, happier than she could remember being in a long time. "We're going to figure this out," she said. "Together."

"Yeah." He pulled her close again and she closed her eyes, content. Love couldn't correct all the mistakes she had made in her life, and it couldn't give her back some of the things she had lost. But for all that Dane challenged her and even annoyed her—or perhaps because of that—she belonged with him. He was the home she had been searching for all these years.

* * * * *

*Look for more books from Cindi Myers
coming soon!*

*And don't miss the previous stories in
The Ranger Brigade: Rocky Mountain Manhunt
miniseries:*

Investigation in Black Canyon
Mountain of Evidence
Mountain Investigation

*Available now wherever Harlequin Intrigue
books are sold!*

COMING NEXT MONTH FROM

ⒽHARLEQUIN
INTRIGUE

Available April 27, 2021

#1995 HER CHILD TO PROTECT
Mercy Ridge Lawmen • by Delores Fossen
When she arrives at a murder scene, Deputy Della Howell is *not* pleased
to find her ex already on the job. After all, she has a secret to keep, one
Sheriff Barrett Logan isn't ready for—she's pregnant with his child. But as they
investigate, sparks reignite. Can they stop the murderer and claim their future?

#1996 THE DECOY
A Kyra and Jake Investigation • by Carol Ericson
A threat is terrorizing the City of Angels—a killer who mimics another killer's MO.
Can LAPD homicide detective Jake McAllister help therapist Kyra Chase solve
crimes in both the past and present before Kyra becomes the next victim?

#1997 KILLER CONSPIRACY
The Justice Seekers • by Lena Diaz
Former First Daughter Harper Manning destroyed Gage Bishop's Secret
Service career. Now she's back with shocking news: their baby lived and is
being held hostage. Gage vows to find and protect the child, but can they also
uncover why their baby's life became part of a conspiracy?

#1998 SUMMER STALKER
A North Star Novel Series • by Nicole Helm
Reece Montgomery's undercover to discover what an unsuspecting B and B
owner knows about her husband's murder. However, when fearless widow
Lianna Kade proposes an ultra-risky plan to lure a killer, it will test Reece's
resolve not to fall for Lianna and her fatherless child.

#1999 INNOCENT HOSTAGE
A Hard Core Justice Thriller • by Juno Rushdan
Their marriage is nearly over. But then Deputy US Marshal Allison Chen-Boyd
and FBI hostage negotiator Henry Boyd learn their eight-year-old son has
been kidnapped. They'll work together—temporarily, of course—to capture the
dangerous cartel hell-bent on vengeance.

#2000 COLD CASE FLASHBACKS
An Unsolved Mystery Book • by Janice Kay Johnson
Twenty-five years after witnessing her mother's murder, Gabriella Ortiz returns
home to face the past she's repressed since childhood. As Gabby's memories
resurface, can Detective Jack Cowan shield her from a killer who is intent on
destroying the future they're hoping to build?

HICNM0421

"Oh, God," she said, the words fighting with her gusting breath. "I need you to take me to the hospital now. I've been shot."

Della forced herself to slow her breathing. Panicking wouldn't help and would only make things worse. Still, it was hard to hold it together when she felt the pain stabbing through her and saw the blood.

The baby.

The fear of losing her child roared through her like an unstoppable train barreling at her. The injury wasn't that serious. Definitely not life-threatening. But any loss of blood could also mean a miscarriage.

Della nearly blurted out for Barrett to hurry, that it wasn't just her arm injury at stake, but there was no need. Barrett was already hurrying, driving as fast as he safely could, and he was doing that while on the phone with Daniel to get his brother and a team out looking for that SUV. And for the men who'd just tried to kill them.

HIEXP0421

For as long as she could remember, she'd wanted to be a cop. And wearing the badge meant facing danger just like this. But everything was different now that her baby was added to the mix. She couldn't lose his child. It didn't matter that the pregnancy hadn't been planned or that Barrett didn't want to be a father. She had to be okay so that her baby would be, too.

She managed to text Jace, to tell him that she and Barrett were heading back to the hospital and that he should do the same. Especially since Daniel would have the pursuit of the gunmen under control. Besides, she wanted Jace at the hospital in case those thugs came after Alice.

"How bad are you hurting?" Barrett asked when he ended the call with Daniel.

Della shook her head, hesitating so that she could try to get control of her voice. "It's okay."

It wasn't, of course. There was pain, but if she tried to describe it to Barrett, she might spill all about the baby. This wasn't the way she wanted him to find out. Later, after she'd been examined. Maybe after the shooters had been caught, she'd tell him then.

Thankfully, they weren't that far from the hospital, only a few minutes, and when Barrett pulled into the parking lot, he drove straight to the doors of the ER. Someone had alerted them, probably Daniel, because the moment Barrett came to a stop, a nurse and an EMT came rushing out toward them. Even though Della could have walked on her own, they put her on a gurney and rushed her into the hospital.

Barrett was right behind them.

Don't miss
Her Child to Protect *by Delores Fossen,*
available May 2021 wherever
Harlequin Intrigue books and ebooks are sold.

Harlequin.com